THE CENTURION

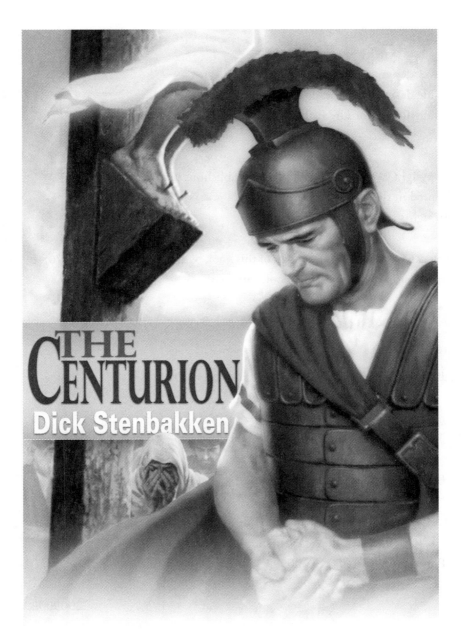

THE CENTURION

Dick Stenbakken

Pacific Press® Publishing Association
Nampa, Idaho
Oshawa, Ontario, Canada
www.pacificpress.com

Cover design by Steve Lanto
Cover design resources from Charles Zingaro
Inside design by Aaron Troia
Inside illustrations by Erik Stenbakken

You can obtain additional copies of this book by calling toll-free 1-800-765-6955
or by visiting www.adventistbookcenter.com.

Library of Congress Cataloging-in-Publication Data

Stenbakken, Dick.
  The centurion / Dick Stenbakken.
    p. cm.
  ISBN 13: 978-0-8163-2332-6 (pbk.)
  ISBN 10: 0-8163-2332-1 (pbk.)
  1. Centurion at the Crucifixion (Biblical figure). 2. Bible.
N.T.—History of Biblical events. I. Title.
  PS3619.T4764767C46 2009
  813'.6—dc22

                                                        2009002967

09 10 11 12 13 • 5 4 3 2 1

DEDICATION

This book is dedicated
to Ardis, who has often been an "operational widow,"
to family members who have offered support and encouragement,
to the chaplains and troops with whom I have served,
and to the glory of the One who changes everyone.

CONTENTS

Introduction..9

Foreword..11

Chapter 1   Into the Battle 13

Chapter 2   Healing Begins 20

Chapter 3   Rewards..28

Chapter 4   The Meeting...36

Chapter 5   Reflections..45

Chapter 6   New Horizons 54

Chapter 7   The Collision..64

Chapter 8   Life Changes 73

Chapter 9   Gaius Becomes an Adult..84

Chapter 10   The Accident 90

Chapter 11   Searching..97

Chapter 12   To Jerusalem 102

Chapter 13   The Augur 108

Chapter 14   Passover..115

Chapter 15   The Visit...121

Chapter 16   The Stage Is Set 128

Chapter 17   Before Pilate 135

Chapter 18   To Herod and Back..143

Chapter 19   The Crucifixion 153

Chapter 20   Meaning, Mercy, and Guard Duty...........................166

Chapter 21   Watching and Waiting...174

Chapter 22   New Beginnings 184

INTRODUCTION

This book is the result of an unfolding series of events set in motion when as a young army chaplain I "accidentally" discovered the awesome power of first-person narrative preaching. I put "accidentally" in quotes because I know that with God there are no accidents: there are, instead, rich insights.

In the course of developing more than sixty biblical narrative sermons, I began to study first-century Roman beliefs, practices, and religious thinking. After all, that was the world in which Jesus and the disciples lived. All those who said, heard, wrote, or read any of the materials we now know as the New Testament were immersed in Roman issues and aspects of life. Roman soldiers and soldiering were all around them, at every street corner and marketplace.

Because of my nearly twenty-four years of active duty as a U.S. Army chaplain, events and narratives involving soldiers naturally drew my attention and deeper study. That even led to my constructing a full set of historically accurate first-century Roman armor and other Roman military gear, some of which is pictured in this book.

The outcome for me personally and professionally continues to be both unfolding and stunning. Looking at the New Testament through first-century Roman eyes has provided me with new insights into the Gospels, Epistles, and other New Testament books. The discoveries—actually epiphanies—began to build, along with eagerness to share the things I had learned. But how to do that? Who could endure a ninety-three-hour-long sermon?

The Centurion

Another epiphany: Jesus told stories . . . stories that called His listeners—and us as readers—to engage with the characters and situations He told about. This book is meant to do the same. While the story is about the centurion who was in charge at the Crucifixion, it is really my story and yours as well. Clothing, customs, and cultures change across time. Human nature and our need for God remain constant. History becomes "His story."

The discussion questions provided for each chapter are intended for individual or group reflections and responses. I strongly encourage you to *write out* your responses in a journal or in the book itself. Written responses call for deeper, more profound discovery than quick verbal or thought responses. However, some answers may be so personal that they are best left written on the heart or lifted to God on the wings of private prayer. That's the reader's call.

If you do read the book and write out answers to the questions posed and conclude at the end of the process that it was a waste of your time, send the book and your written responses to me, and I will personally refund your purchase price—no questions asked.

So, here's the challenge: get into the skin and daily life of the centurion, and experience the life-changing power of Jesus.

Dick Stenbakken
2493 Frances Drive
Loveland, Colorado 80537

FOREWORD

Dick Stenbakken brings Bible characters to life. His ability to resurrect ancient Bible personalities through first-person narratives amazes me. His presentations at the U.S. Senate received rave reviews as he transported his listeners back into Bible times with gifted narrations. I urged him to capture these experiences in print. Finally, his wonderful centurion has been brought to life on the printed page.

Benefitting from Dr. Stenbakken's decades of military service as well as his imagination and biblical knowledge, you will meet Longinus, the centurion. Dick, a retired army colonel, will enable you to follow Longinus's journey from his entry into a Roman legion at age eighteen until this centurion witnesses Jesus' crucifixion and resurrection. I enthusiastically recommend this book.

Barry Black, PhD
Chaplain of the United States Senate

Chapter 1

INTO THE BATTLE

A damp, bone-chilling breeze filtered through the trees as Longinus peered warily over a large gray rock formation at the edge of the thick, dark forest. Beyond the rocks lay an open, fog-shrouded field. The first rays of dawn promised both the warmth of the sun and the heat of battle.

Although he couldn't see them yet, he and the other Roman troops knew that the barbarians were there—waiting, planning, and eager for a fight. He had yet to encounter these "savages," as his commander called them, but he had heard others say that they were giants.

"They're fierce and fearless," said a fellow soldier. "They're without culture, mercy, or fear—savages!"

And . . . *they were out there.* He could hear them but couldn't see them through the swirling fog on the grassy meadow. *Are they as fierce and powerful as others say? Or does fear make them seem larger than life?* He would soon know.

As the rays of the rising sun melted away the fog, Longinus and the others heard the *cornu* (the large, round battle-signal horn) calling them to assemble. Instantly, more than six hundred Roman soldiers formed into ranks of twelve men each. At the next notes of the *cornu,* each group of twelve formed into the *testudo* ("turtle"). The formation did, indeed, look like a large, menacing turtle.

Longinus had to smile to himself at the thought. He remembered the day when he was a new recruit and a tough-as-iron instructor had said, "Today, you will learn how to form a turtle." He'd laughed to himself then. *Turtle?* he'd thought. *I want to fight, not lumber along like a dumb turtle!* The instructor had glared at Longinus as though reading his thoughts and had growled, "Just do as I say, or you'll have welts all over your body. Now, form up three across and four deep—and do it on the double!"

After what seemed like hundreds of attempts, they did learn the *testudo* formation that day. The first three recruits across the front were taught to hold their shields at eye level and their swords at the right edge of each shield. When they were doing this to the satisfaction of their trainer, he had the remaining nine members of the formation put their shields over their own heads and the heads of those in front of them, forming a type of roof or protective shell over the group. The "turtle" was now complete.

They had practiced the formation over and over until their arms ached from holding the shields and swords. Their wicker practice shields and wooden swords were twice the weight of the real gear.

"It builds character and stamina," barked the trainer whenever anyone dared to show stress from the exertion. "This is just practice," he'd said. "Someday, it will be real. Perfect it now, because when the time comes, your response will need to be automatic. You won't have time to think about it. You need to know how to do it immediately, or you'll wind up as food for the vultures."

Now the words of that rugged trainer echoed in Longinus's head. The time had indeed arrived. This was for real. Now Longinus would prove himself. He was determined to earn the recognition and acceptance he'd longed for all of his life, or he would literally die trying. He had no intent of becoming fodder for vultures.

The *cornu* sounded sharp, ear-piercing notes again, and the formation closed ranks as if they were one man. Each drew his sword in his right hand and thrust it to his right, out beyond the shield. They closed ranks tightly, until there was a solid line of bright, blood-red shields forming a sword-pierced wall of death. Those in the front of each rank wore greaves on their legs as additional protection.

The early morning sun danced from each bronze hand-protecting boss at the center of the shields and glimmered from the shields' bronze-reinforced edges. It was an awesome and fearful sight. With the polished swords thrusting out between the shields, the formation gave the appearance of an angry, metal-studded porcupine.

Each rank of twelve soldiers stood next to another and another and another. The "turtles" were ready to move, but not at a turtle's pace. Theirs would be a rapidly moving, noisy, intimidating wall of death, pressing into the barbarian lines.

Billhooks, agricultural tools used to trim trees and cut brush, were also used as weapons.

As the Roman troops awaited the next trumpet order, Longinus could taste the metallic flavor of fear in his mouth. His heart sounded like a drum beating rapidly behind the metal-banded armor covering his chest.

The enemy was just becoming visible. They, too, were in a line formation. They carried smaller shields and a wide variety of swords, spears, bows, billhooks, and clubs at the ready. No doubt about it—they weren't going to run. They would *fight*.

So be it, he thought. *I'm trained, equipped, and ready.*

Suddenly, the barbarians began to shout, curse, and howl like animals as they rushed forward in a mad, death-defying charge. They sounded like a herd of wild horses stampeding down a gravel road.

Longinus tightened his grip on both his shield and sword. As he did, the *cornu* sounded for the legionnaires to charge. The wall of armored Roman soldiers moved steadily toward the barbarians, their measured steps in cadence with the sound of their swords slapping the metal edges of their shields.

As the Roman troops marched forward, the barbarians released a volley of arrows at them. The volley was split: some arrows were aimed directly at the Roman line, while hundreds of others were launched upward in high arcs intended to rain down death from above upon the Romans.

The Centurion

Longinus instinctively hunkered down, pulling his chin low, his shoulders up, and his shield a bit higher. Now, only a three-inch window remained between the top of his shield and the forehead-guard on his helmet. The red-and-yellow painted shield covered everything from his eyes to just below his knees. Since he was in the first rank, his legs were protected by greaves. He hated them. They were extra weight, and unless they were adjusted correctly, the bulky things dug into his feet.

The barbarian arrows thumped against his shield. Their iron points stuck in the multilayered wooden shield, but didn't penetrate far enough to do any damage. The shield worked! Longinus was glad for that. He felt an arrow glance off his right greave. As it bounced harmlessly away, he instantly reevaluated the value of his greaves. *OK,* he thought. *I guess they're a good idea after all!*

The two lines of warriors crashed into each other with ear-splitting violence. The Romans held their line, pushing with their shields and jabbing with their swords. And now, Roman arrows rained down on the barbarians, who were caught off guard because they were trying to defend themselves from the sword thrusts of the front line of Roman soldiers. The flashing Roman arrows brought many of them down immediately.

The *cornu* sounded another order, and the soldiers in the turtle formation brought their shields down to eye level and formed several layers of "front lines." As one group of Romans threw their spears, they took a step to the side and backward, and the next line of Roman soldiers then stepped forward to throw their spears. The overlapping and rotating lines allowed the Romans to advance, defend, and throw hundreds of lead-weighted, needle-sharp spears at the barbarians—and more of them fell. The legion had its losses too. Longinus saw a soldier to his left cut down with a spear to his throat. *Keep your shield up!* his inner voice screamed.

Above the din and confusion of the battle, Longinus heard the unmistakable, gravel-coarse voice of his centurion, barking commands just to the left of where Longinus stood. At the sound of that voice, he instinctively shifted his eyes toward his commander. What he saw in that rapid glance made his blood run cold.

The commander had turned around to gesture to the legionnaires positioned near a large stand of trees. Out of the sight of the distracted Roman commander and that of the soldiers he was addressing, two barbarians slunk from behind some large rocks and dashed directly at him. They were about to cut down the unsuspecting Roman commander.

Longinus shouted, "Julius! Left! Now!"

His long-time best friend and fellow soldier saw immediately what was about to happen. Both Julius and Longinus sprinted toward their centurion and the rapidly approaching barbarians. One of the barbarians saw them coming and took a defensive stand meant to delay them, while the other barbarian continued to close the distance between himself and the unsuspecting centurion.

The shouts and the sound of running caused the commander to wheel around just as the barbarian hurled his spear. The fortunately timed turn caused the spear to miss the Roman leader's body by inches. It did, however, nick his arm.

Longinus and Julius struggled to bring down the barbarian who was blocking their access to the commander. Julius finally subdued him as Longinus sprinted to the aid of his centurion, who was now in a hand-to-hand struggle with a barbarian who outweighed him by eighty pounds.

With a swing of his tree-trunk-sized arm, the barbarian knocked the centurion to the ground and thrust a second spear at him. The centurion rolled desperately away, and the weapon pinned his tunic to the dirt. The barbarian unleashed a savage kick that made the centurion double over in pain, gasping for what he thought might be his last breath. The barbarian smirked as he raised the spear for the final thrust.

At that instant, Longinus threw his spear and caught the barbarian in the ribs. With a shrill shriek, the barbarian clutched at his side and dropped his own weapon. Longinus was on him instantly, with Julius right behind. The wounded barbarian struggled, but he was no match for two strapping Roman soldiers. They used their swords to end the wild, thrashing struggle.

Then Longinus and Julius turned their attention to their commander, who had managed to get up onto one knee and was gasping for breath.

"Sir! Are you all right?" queried Longinus, as he reached out to steady the shaken man.

"Yes, I think so. Good work, soldiers," he gasped as he struggled to his feet. "Good work, indeed. I never saw them coming. It was a well-set trap, and I almost wound up being the mouse," he said with a bit of a smile.

"Longinus and Julius, right?" asked the centurion, nodding his head toward them.

"Yes, sir," replied the two soldiers in unison.

The Centurion

"You saved my life today. I won't forget that. You will be amply rewarded," the centurion said as he examined the wound on his arm. "I'm in your debt, and I thank you for doing your job well. Now, back to your positions. We have a battle to win." With that, he turned and began to direct the rest of the troops.

Longinus and Julius grinned at each other like a couple of schoolboys who had just won a prize. They had saved their commander's life, and he'd said he would reward them. What's more, the commander actually knew their names. They mattered.

That's why Longinus was here. He had wanted—and won—the recognition of his commander. For an instant, that recognition nearly erased his fear.

Then, suddenly, out of nowhere, a huge, ragged, wild-eyed enemy lurched directly toward him. The man wore no armor and carried only a small round shield and a huge wooden club with iron studs protruding from it. His shock of unruly auburn hair made him look like a moving torch. The snarl on his face made clear that he was inflamed with hatred and rage and intended to offer Longinus to the vultures. His eyes locked on to Longinus's eyes. At that instant, everything seemed to both speed up and slow down. Time slipped into a new dimension.

As the barbarian crashed into Longinus's shield, Longinus swiftly shoved the shield out and up. The shield caught the man just under the chin, ripping a ragged red gash in his neck. His eyes widened with pain and surprise. Longinus made a quick thrust with his sword that dug deep into his opponent's side. The man roared with anger and pain and began to fall. As he fell, he grabbed Longinus's shield and kicked his legs out from under Longinus, putting him on his hands and knees. Then the huge barbarian swung his massive foot up, catching Longinus full in the face. The blow sent Longinus sprawling onto his back while the barbarian sprang to his feet.

Longinus's shield was gone, and—the wind knocked out of him—he couldn't lift his sword. He rolled over and tried to get up, but the huge foot of the barbarian thumped down on his armor, pinning him to the ground. If he had not been wearing the new, banded armor, the barbarian would have crushed his chest like a man stepping on a beetle.

Then, Longinus saw, as if in slow motion, the barbarian bringing down his huge war club. The blow was intended to crush Longinus's skull. Instinctively,

Longinus raised both hands to ward off the impending impact. As he did, he jerked his head to the side, attempting to avoid the worst of the blow.

When the club hit, Longinus could both feel and hear the bones in his left arm break. Then the club slammed into his helmet with a resounding crash. Immediately, Longinus's vision was filled with spinning, cloudy darkness that was spangled and split with flashes of brilliant light and a swirling, red mist. The sound of voices of men in combat all around him changed to a roar like that of a waterfall plunging over a rock face. He thought, *So this is what it feels like to die!*

Then everything went black and silent.

Questions for Thought and Discussion

1. Who or what are your "savages" or threats? What are your current fears? What are your emotional or spiritual battles? How do you fight those personal threats? How can you know their true strength?
2. The *testudo* formation gave maximum protection for all members. What group could help sustain and protect you? How do they do that? What do you contribute to the group? Who needs *your* protection?
3. Roman soldiers listened to the battle trumpet, the *cornu,* for directives. How do you "hear" God's marching orders for your spiritual battles?
4. When have you had your spiritual or emotional shield pulled down? What was it like to be vulnerable, and how did you handle it?
5. Have you faced the reality of your own death? What affect did it have on you to face your own mortality?
6. How and from whom do you seek approval?

Chapter 2

HEALING BEGINS

Longinus heard a voice calling his name. The voice sounded strange, yet familiar—like someone calling to him from a windswept mountaintop.

"Longinus! Longinus! Can you hear me?"

Well, yes, he could, but it didn't seem important to answer. Not right then, at least.

Longinus felt as though he were both present and absent. He heard the voice but either couldn't or didn't want to respond. He felt a spinning, swirling, twisting sensation, like being in a small boat drifting and bobbing on a river, or like a feather floating on an updraft. Real—but not real. Present—but absent at the same time.

The voice interrupted his thoughts. "Longinus! Longinus! Open your eyes—speak to me!" The voice was insistent, demanding, irritating. "Longinus, it's Julius! Open your eyes!"

Julius? Julius? What is he doing floating down this river too? Curiosity and irritation forced Longinus to open his eyes. When he did, the brightness was intense, sharp, and painful. It felt as though someone was sticking his finger in his eye while hitting his head with a club at the same time. The sensation was painfully nauseating.

With a start, he remembered the war club headed for his face. His eyes widened in terror, but there was no club, no barbarian, no sound of battle—only the wild thumping of his heart, like a drum banging in his ears. Julius was kneeling over him, trying to wipe his face with a wet cloth. Longinus recoiled from the cloth, jerking his head away. As he did, a wave of dizziness and pain took his breath away.

"Take it easy, Longinus. You'll be all right. You're safe. We got him. Your sword work slowed him down, and my spear finished him. It's over. We won the battle.

"He had you down flat. The first blow was pretty bad; I could see that," Julius continued. "He raised the club again to finish you off. That's when I got him with my spear. He was a big, tough savage, but we did it. Together, we got him! Now let's get you some medical help."

As Longinus tried to get up, he felt even more dizzy and disoriented, and he felt as thought a winepress were crushing his left arm. It jutted out at an odd angle; his arm wasn't where it should be.

Julius helped him sit up. "Here, my friend," he encouraged, "drink some of this wine—it will ease your pain."

Roman canteens were made of bronze and iron and were lined with wax to keep the contents free of rust. They more often held wine than water.

The Centurion

Longinus never had liked the taste of wine, but he liked pain even less, so he drank slowly from Julius's canteen. The wine was horrible, but his thirst was like a raging fire, and the liquid helped quench both the thirst and the pain.

"Longinus, tell me—what's the name of the emperor? Who is our centurion? What year is it?"

"Look, Julius," huffed Longinus, "I took a real hit, but my brains aren't scrambled yet. I'm putting the pieces together, I'll be fine. Just help me to my feet and give me a little time."

"All right, I can do that," Julius said. "But answer my questions. Who is the emperor? And what is the name of our centurion?"

"Why do you keep asking those silly questions? Did some barbarian slam you on the head too?" Longinus said with a half smile, half grimace.

"Well?"

"If it will make you feel better, I do know the answer to both of your questions," replied Longinus. "The emperor is Augustus—Caesar the August . . . the god. And our centurion—whose life we just saved—is . . . is . . . hmmm. Who is he?"

"Come on, Longinus, you're just playing with me . . . aren't you?"

"Yes," Longinus said with a snicker. "Our centurion is Pontius Pilate—'the spear from the sea.' We saved his hide earlier today, and he promised to reward us for that. There. Did I pass the test?"

"You sure did, and I'm glad. I always knew you had a hard head. It seems to have served you well today! Now, let's have the medical group take a look at you. Maybe you'll even live long enough to collect on the reward Pilate promised us!"

Julius gently helped Longinus stand up. "We need to get that arm looked at. And you have quite a cut where your helmet hit your head," commented Julius. "That barbarian would have crushed your skull like an egg if it hadn't been for your helmet."

Longinus was wobbly on his feet. "You'll have to help me get to the medical tent. My arm is killing me. I could hear the bone break when the club hit my arm. Then everything just went out like a candle in the wind. He must have really pounded me.

"You saved my life. I thought for sure I was going to be buzzard bait. How can I ever repay you?"

"Here, lean on me," Julius said. "We're brothers in battle. You've helped me, and now it was my turn to help you. Don't worry about repayment. Just worry about getting those wounds cared for."

Walking was not as easy as Longinus thought it would be. The forest began to spin, the earth beneath his sandals seemed to be moving, and his legs felt as limber as green willow branches. He was glad to have Julius to lean on. The swelling and discoloration in his left arm spoke clearly of a broken bone or worse. Fortunately, the arm was partially numb from the wound and the wine. But he knew that would change.

The unit had professional medical personnel—doctors who had received training at one of the many different military medical schools. The doctors and their helpers were busy and businesslike as they tended to the wounds of the legion's troops. The more severely wounded were treated first, and then those who had less life-threatening problems. The medical tent was larger than the eight-man *contubernium* tents used to house the troops when they were on the march.

Medical and surgical instruments were arrayed in wooden cases and grouped according to their use. In one case were short saws used to amputate limbs too badly mangled to be restored. Longinus had encountered veterans who had experienced amputation and lived to tell about it. He looked at his arm, then at the saws, and fervently hoped the two would never meet.

Another case held bronze scalpels used for surgery and the removal of arrows or spears. Strands of hemp cord were available to help staunch bleeding. And cots raised on platforms kept the wounded at a comfortable working level for the medical people as they tended to their charges.

Grouped by the severity of their wounds or illnesses, the patients would be assigned to various tented areas for aftercare. The Roman doctors had long ago learned to put their facilities on high and dry ground to prevent a contagious sickness known as "bad air." The Latin term was *mal airia*. The physicians had also learned to sterilize their instruments and to isolate those with contagious illnesses from those who were wounded.

Longinus had early recognized the benefits offered by the doctors in camp. He had assisted when one of his tent mates was ill, and he was impressed by the skill of the doctors. Now, he was the patient and glad he had observed enough medical care to trust the doctors who would be treating him.

The Centurion

Not long after they got to the medical tent, Longinus was offered a seat and was told the physician would see him shortly. When a physician arrived, he took one look at Longinus's arm and began to probe gently with his fingers to see where the break was. "Let me know when it hurts," he said.

As the doctor examined his arm, Longinus felt bolts of pain so sharp that he gasped, clenched his teeth, and then grabbed Julius's arm. "That must be where the break is," the doctor said as he saw Longinus's reaction. "It's definitely broken. I'll put a splint on it to help it heal. But first, I have to close the wound on your arm."

Longinus knew what was coming next. He had helped hold down other soldiers while this procedure took place. It was painful but successful. He watched as the doctor took a thin piece of bronze wire, cut a short piece, and then sharpened one end. The doctor repeated this until he had prepared five pieces of wire. Once that was done, the physician held the wire in a flame for a moment until it glowed. After dipping it in wine to cool it, he began to use the wire as a suture.

"Here, soldier," said the doctor, "bite on this piece of wood while I close the wound. It won't help the pain, but it will keep you from breaking a tooth or biting through your tongue. I'll splint your arm once the wires are in place."

Longinus wanted to watch—and he didn't want to watch. But his fascination with the process compelled him to look at what the doctor was doing. After cleaning the wound with wine and putting ointment on it, the doctor deftly pierced one side of the wound with the sharpened wire, ran it under the skin, across the wound, and through the good flesh beyond it. Then he pulled the skin together, and bent the other end of the wire over, tightening the lacerated edges of flesh together with the wire suture. When he had closed the wound with the other four pieces of wire, he quickly and deftly covered it with a cloth bandage and then made a splint of short, thin pieces of wood and bound them in place with another cloth.

The process was less painful than Longinus had imagined. Maybe it was due to the wine the doctor used to clean the gash, or maybe just the wine he'd had to drink. Either way, he was grateful for the obvious skill and compassion of the doctor.

"The good news is that your head wound is not that bad," the doctor commented. "You'll have a scar from that wound, but that's about all. All it will require is a cloth compress that you'll need to have changed periodically.

"Keep your arm in a sling, and get plenty of rest. Come back tomorrow, and I'll change the dressings. You can expect the arm to swell and hurt. There will be some bleeding from the cut on your head, but you should be fine and fit for duty within a few weeks. It will take that long for the bones in your arm to heal. You were fortunate that the break was clean and that the bone didn't displace badly."

Well, fortunate *is a relative word,* Longinus thought to himself. *At least I'm alive. Hurting as never before—but alive.* That was something. Quite a big something, he decided, pain or not.

Longinus was glad the ordeal was over. He found a leather strap and made a sling for his arm, glad that he was free to go back to his tent. Julius helped steady him as they made their way to their quarters.

Longinus knew he wouldn't be tempted to use his arm. He could feel the pain with each step and each heartbeat. The only good thing was that the pain reminded him that he was still alive. So, in a perverse way, the pain was welcome.

Julius insisted that Longinus have several more long sips of wine. *Nasty stuff,* thought Longinus. He couldn't understand why people wanted to drink the bitter liquid. However, the wine did dull his pain. He appreciated that.

Longinus was absolutely exhausted. It didn't take long for him to drift off to sleep. But then, suddenly, he awoke, his eyes wide with terror. Then he realized he'd had a nightmare. He'd been dreaming that the barbarian wasn't really dead after all—that Julius had only wounded him, and now the guy was back and clearly bent on finishing Longinus off. In the dream, the barbarian was twisting Longinus's wounded arm in an attempt to repay Longinus for the pain he'd inflicted on him.

Longinus heard himself scream in terror. His tent mates, and Julius in particular, rushed to his cot to assure him he wasn't in danger. Then Longinus realized that he had turned over in his sleep and pinned his arm against the cot. The pain was real—the nightmare was not. But it had seemed as real as the event itself. The barbarian's face was etched in his memory and was far, far too real and too present.

The Centurion

Longinus had been in battle before, but this was the first time he had encountered death eye to eye. He had looked into the eyes of a man who intended to kill him—who had tried to kill him and very nearly *had* killed him. Longinus had stared back at the man as he tried to kill him before he was killed. Now he knew what it was like to look death full in the face up close. It was quite different from throwing a spear at an enemy or sending an arrow speeding to destroy someone. Face-to-face combat was more intimate. More memorable. More profoundly personal. More deeply disturbing.

Longinus knew that somehow every moment of life ahead of him would always be more precious, more meaningful, and more appreciated than ever before. The sky would be a deeper blue, the air more refreshingly crisp, and the sunrise and sunsets more color-saturated and intense. He would appreciate common things more.

He had peered through the iron gates of death, turned around, and walked back toward life. It was as if something or Someone was pulling him toward a new reality.

Death had changed life. Forever.

Questions for Thought and Discussion

1. The Roman helmet was designed to provide maximum protection for the head and brain. The devil attacks our minds, our emotions, and our morals. How do you protect yourself from his attacks?
2. Have you ever been wounded to the point where you could not function independently? What was that like for you? Whom did you lean on for help? Who needs to lean on you for help right now? What will you do to help that person? When and how will you do it?
3. How hard or easy is it for you to give help to someone in need? How hard or easy is it for you to receive help from others? Which is easier for you to do? Explain.
4. When have you experienced the probing of the Holy Spirit in your life to find and correct brokenness in you? On a scale of 1 to 10 (10 being the maximum), how comfortable was that experience? What were the results?

5. Recount a time or experience when things could have turned out very badly for you but instead turned out very well. Who or what made the difference?

6. What experiences in your life helped change your focus so that common things became profound and the ordinary became extraordinary? How did those experiences change you in other ways?

Chapter 3

REWARDS

Two days after Longinus had been wounded, he and Julius were eating together with the other six soldiers assigned to their eight-man *contubernium* at the edge of the military camp. The two soldiers were surprised when they spotted a runner from the command section approaching. The messenger inquired for Longinus and Julius. "That would be us," Julius responded. "What can we do for you?"

The runner replied, "You are both to report to the commander immediately."

"Why? What did we do?" queried Longinus.

"I don't know," the runner said. "But orders are orders."

The two soldiers looked at each other, wondering what this could be about. Longinus's arm had become infected, and he was pretty weak and wobbly on his feet. "I guess you'll have to go alone," he told Julius. "I hope we haven't done something wrong."

"I don't think so," the runner said. "Pilate seemed to be in a good mood—much better than earlier in the day. At dawn, he had a soldier flogged for breaking ranks in the battle a couple of days ago, but he seemed pleased when he sent me to fetch you two."

Somehow, Julius didn't find that very comforting. Flogging was a brutal business—so brutal that it was unlawful to flog a woman or a Roman citizen. That form of punishment was reserved for the non-Roman—a slave, or in this case, a soldier who deserted his post. Julius had seen the whip flay the skin off a person's back. Lead weights in the leather straps of the whip acted like claws, ripping the flesh open at each stroke. People often died when they were flogged. Those who didn't usually wished—even begged—for death. Not a pleasant thought to contemplate after what the runner had said what had happened that morning.

As Julius and Longinus looked at each other, wondering what the summons was all about, the runner turned on his heel and said over his shoulder, "You have been summoned to report within the next ten minutes, so don't delay. I've given you the message and will report that to Pilate."

With that, the runner strode off, the gravel crunching under his sandals.

"I guess I'd better go and see what this is about." Julius was thinking out loud. "I'll report back as soon as I can."

"I better go too," moaned Longinus. "We were both summoned."

"No, I'll go and represent you. Surely our centurion has heard about your injuries and will understand that you have been ordered not to move about unless it is to go back to the medical tent," Julius said. "Stay here for now. If you must be there too, I'll come back and help you get there. I'll have to run to make it there on time as it is. You'd never make it anyway."

"That's true," agreed Longinus. "You better go quickly. I'll stay here. Hurry back and let me know what's going on."

Julius wiped his mouth, straightened his tunic, smoothed his hair as best he could, and began to jog toward the commander's tent.

Longinus leaned back on his bed and thought about the past days. The cut on his head was healing well. The arm was another matter. It would take more time.

Another wound needed healing too, one he couldn't touch—one the doctor couldn't bandage. It had to do with the inner man—with his personal brush with death and the close-up killing of the barbarian. *Sure, it is combat. You expect death to be all around you. But this is different somehow,* he reflected.

Longinus's mind wandered to the panoply of Roman gods. He wondered if perhaps the gods had spared his life for some special purpose. Many Romans considered Augustus, the emperor, to be a son of the gods. In fact, Augustus had long called himself the *divi filius*—the son of god—and had been proclaimed *Pater Patriae,* "The Father of the Fatherland."

The Centurion

Longinus recalled when he had taken the military oath—the *sacramentum*. That event had strong religious overtones, to the point that the spirit of the oath, the *genius sacramenti*, was often worshiped. And, he reflected, the sacred standards of the unit were kept in a shrine, or *aedes*, in the middle of the camp. Many of the soldiers venerated Mithra, the Persian deity who offered adherents the promise of life after death; or the storm god, Dolichenus, whom the Romans called Jupiter; or the god of war, Mars. He might need to look more deeply into these matters of worship.

Longinus's reverie was interrupted by Julius's return. Julius's expression failed to reveal whether the interview with Pontius Pilate had brought good news or bad news. It was clear, however, that Julius could hardly contain whatever it was—yet at the same time was holding it back.

"Well?"

"Well, what?" Julius teased.

"Don't play games. What happened?"

Julius broke into a broad grin. "You'll never believe it!"

"I suppose not, especially since I have no idea what happened."

Julius began to excitedly report the encounter with Pilate, their centurion. "When I got to the commander's tent, the guard stopped me and wouldn't let me in until I told him I'd been instructed to report to Pilate. Longinus, you'll never guess who the guard on duty was."

"Since there are about two hundred possibilities, no, I couldn't," responded Longinus a bit impatiently. "Do you want to let me in on the secret, or do I have to spend the next month guessing?"

"None other than your old friend, Pulcher."

"Pulcher? You can't mean that irritating, pain-of-a-person Plutonius Pulcher, who was with us in basic training!"

"The very same."

"I thought he'd have been thrown out of the army a long time ago, right on his face," Longinus said derisively.

"So, you do remember him," laughed Julius.

"Remember him! How could I ever forget him?" shot back Longinus with eyes blazing. "Why, he threatened me every day of training for weeks. He was like a sandbur in my sandal.

"Do you remember the time we were standing in line for inspection and Pulcher pushed me with his foot? I landed like a wounded bird right in front of Aquinas! That cost me four extra days of work in the kitchen! Then there was the time we were being paid in coins, and he 'bumped' me, sending all my coins scattering like the leaves of autumn. And the time when the commander asked for volunteers to clean out the latrine, and he prodded me in the back with his spear, causing me to jump forward a step—and the commander thanked me for volunteering! And then he stole my rations and replaced them with rocks when we were on that twenty-seven-mile march—and I didn't notice until we stopped to eat. He laughed and ate *my* food and shared it with others while I starved. I've *never* disliked anyone so intensely. He has all the warmth of a snake. What's he doing here?"

"He just transferred in," Julius replied. "Since they had no place for him immediately, they put him on guard duty. Today's rotation put him at the gate of the commander's compound. It looks as if he'll be in the unit with us."

"As if I don't have enough pain already—now this!" Longinus complained. "Maybe you should have let the barbarian finish me off! Pulcher is *always* a problem. I can't stand even the thought of him, let alone the idea that he may wind up in our unit. He's the most foul-mouthed, ugly spirited, coarsest person I've ever met. Now he's here. Unbelievable—utterly unbelievable!"

"Well," responded Julius, "I know that the two of you didn't hit it off, but—"

"Hit it off! Do you remember when we were first learning to use our swords? They gave us those heavy wooden ones—the *clava*—to practice with. You were there when he nearly broke my ribs with his. I mean, it was *practice,* and he smashed that thing into me like he was trying to make a window in my ribs that a crow could fly through. It was downhill from there. Pulcher the pain. He's back, like a repeating nightmare. I can't believe it. Great! Thanks. I really needed that bit of news," snorted Longinus derisively.

"There's more," said Julius. "Do you want to hear it?"

"After hearing about Pulcher and mixing it up with that barbarian, I'm ready for anything," moaned Longinus. "So, did you get past 'the pain' to see Pilate?"

"I sure did."

"And?"

"Pilate said he was being assigned back to Rome. He's leaving tomorrow, but he wanted to follow up on our 'saving his hide,' as he called it. He thanked me—really us—for what we did. He even asked how you were doing."

The silver *denarius* comprised a day's wages for a Roman soldier. The front of this one shows Augustus, who ruled from 27 B.C. to A.D.14. The back shows Caius and Lucius Caesar.

"Wow, you actually got into the commander's quarters! I would have loved to have been there. So, tell me, what was it like?"

"Not as fancy as I thought it might be, but very, very nice. He actually has a big polished wood table and leather-covered chairs and bronze oil lamps all around for light. And he has quite a collection of maps and scrolls too. With your bent for reading, you would have loved that. I've never seen so many scrolls."

"What else?" questioned Longinus.

"Are you ready for this?" Julius grinned.

"After being nearly clubbed to death by that barbarian and now finding out about Pulcher, I guess I can handle it. Try me. What now?" asked Longinus with a raised eyebrow.

"Pilate gave us sixty days off!"

"Sixty days' leave? That's great! What about our pay? I have to replace my helmet, and I still owe for my armor. I don't want to go broke."

Julius held up two identical bulging leather bags.

"Yes, sixty days off—*with pay! And MORE!* Here, look in your bag. Pilate said it would help us enjoy the leave time more."

When Longinus opened his bag, he was astonished to see a double handful of sparkling new silver *denarii*. His eyes went wide at the sight of what he quickly guessed to be more than a year's wages.

"This is way more than sixty days' pay!"

Julius just laughed at his friend. "We've been very richly rewarded. Pilate wrote out orders authorizing us to stay at a villa in Saalburg and to have free and full use of the hot springs there. He said it would help your healing before you return to duty. And that's not all!"

"There's more? Please don't tell me that Pulcher is going too!"

"Forget Pulcher," laughed Julius. "We've both been promoted. Effective today! And to mark our promotion and as a token of his personal thanks, Pilate gave us identical carved signet rings with the imperial Roman eagle on them. Here's yours." Julius grinned as he held out his hand with a new bronze ring in it.

Longinus flushed with excitement. He had always longed for recognition. He'd always wanted appreciation. That was one of the reasons he had left his father's leather-working shop. He had realized there was no hope for recognition or appreciation and no future in his small, poverty-stricken home village. So when he turned seventeen, he begged his father to let him join the Roman legions.

His father hadn't been willing to release him though. "Do you think marching with the soldiers will be a better life than the one you have here?" he'd shot back. "No. I need you here. I won't allow you to leave. You'll stay here and help me, you thankless pup. After all the food I've given you, it's time you paid me back with sweat. Get back to your bench before I use this leather strap on you."

According to Roman law, that was that—period. Fathers were practically gods. As long as they were alive, the children could do nothing, decide *nothing*, on their own. Sons couldn't choose their own lifework, their jobs, or even their own wife. The Roman father did all of that. The son's place was to give absolute, unquestioning obedience.

And if a son offended his father, the father could disown the son and adopt another. Then the natural-born son would have no rights, no standing—nothing. He would be an outcast in society. So, Longinus had to obey his father. There was no alternative. He stayed. He worked. He waited.

A year later, Longinus finally talked his father into releasing him to join the legions. At eighteen, he was, according to his father, "eating more than he was worth." His father sent him off with the farewell words, "Good riddance. Leave—and don't look back. Let the army feed you. Maybe they can make something worthwhile of your worthless hide. When you walk out the door, know that I have officially and forever disowned you."

It wasn't exactly a heartwarming departure, but at least Longinus received permission from his father to join the legions. That was all that mattered.

And now?

A smile crept across Longinus's face, as he thought, *If only Father could see me now! A soldier. A respected, richly rewarded, newly promoted soldier with a signet ring given to me by my commander! I have in my hand more silver than my father will ever see the rest of his life, working in that dump of a leather shop—more recognition than he will ever get, more value than he could imagine.*

Yes, Longinus smiled as he thought of it, the sensation was sweet. He was respected, rewarded, successful, and promoted. Things were going to be just fine. Maybe the gods were smiling on him, after all.

The only cloud was that putrid Pulcher. But why let *that* annoying pest spoil his reward? Sixty days of paid leave, an early promotion, a beautiful ring, and a year's wages in silver. Life was good. It would be a fantastic sixty days—Longinus was sure of that.

He had a future. He had transitioned from being a regular soldier, to being a wounded warrior, and then a well-off, worthy, newly promoted soldier. Life couldn't be better.

Questions for Thought and Discussion

1. What is the best reward, award, or recognition you have ever received? What was it like for you to have that level of recognition? What was it like for those around you?
2. Who would be glad if you gave them a reward or recognition? What would have the most positive impact? How and when can you bring that reward to reality?
3. Are inner wounds more challenging to heal than physical wounds?

How? How can spirituality help heal both kinds of wounds? Recount when you either received or participated in either of those kinds of healing.

4. Relate how you might respond (as a first-century Roman) if you heard Jesus describe God as our Father. What kind of relationship did/do you have with your parents—particularly, your father? Describe how that affects your relationships with your nuclear family, your work family, and your worship family. What kind of Father is God for you?

5. What are the implications of the concept of being adopted by God, given the understanding of adoption in the Roman world? What is the impact for you today? Ponder the following texts from the mind-set of a first-century Roman: Matthew 6:9; Luke 12:32; John 5:19, 30; 6:38–40; 16:27; John 20:17; Romans 8:15–17, 22, 23.

6. Have you had or do you have a Pulcher in your life? How do you deal with negative or destructive persons without allowing them to drag you into negative thoughts, emotions, comments, or actions?

Chapter 4

THE MEETING

Saalburg was more beautiful than Longinus could ever have imagined. The Roman fort was quite small and had been built as part of the frontier protection system that extended all along the empire's border. The whole system was known as the *limes*. The countryside surrounding Saalburg was tree covered, with softly rolling hills and open green fields that provided a variety of colors and textures.

Among the area's attractions were the hot springs and spa at Bad Homburg, not far from the Roman fort. That was the destination of choice for Longinus and Julius. Saalburg was just a nearby place where they could stay while on their extended leave. Food and lodging would be provided for them by the commander at Saalburg, since they were on official orders. That would save them the expense of paying for food and lodging in the community—a significant savings.

Longinus had, of course, visited the community baths in Rome. There, the water was heated by fires built under the marble floors of the baths. Elaborate systems of tunnels and stone ductwork spread the warmth through the whole building. Because the various bathing waters and also the public toilets adjacent to the bathing areas used lead pipes to move the water, the system of piping became known as plumbing, from the Latin word for lead—*plumbum*.

The baths of Rome were truly an engineering marvel. Of course, the baths there, as in other places, were not only for bathing; they were the cultural center of the community—a place to meet, greet, and exchange ideas, news, and rumors.

In the spas built by the Romans, the baths were divided into three main areas: the steaming hot *caldarium,* the more moderate *tepidarium,* and the much cooler waters known as the *frigidarium.* A visitor to the baths could move from the steamy *caldarium* to the *tepidarium* and then have a delightful swim in the cooler pool. The water at Bad Homburg was as clear as the air, so it was impossible to estimate how deep the pools were. Pebbles on the bottom seemed to be only inches from the surface. And as bubbles rose through the water, they caused it to sparkle, making the pool's surface look as if it were dancing.

The *strigil,* made of bronze, bone, or ivory, was used to scrape grime and dead skin from the body after a hot bath.

Though the natural hot springs of Bad Homburg were a bit different from the heated pools in Rome, the bathing process was the same. Because the Romans had no bath soap, bathers would begin by going into the hottest pool and working up a sweat. Next, they would rub scented oil all over their bodies. Then they would take a curved and polished bone or metal instrument called a *strigil* and use it to scrape away the dead skin and grime that had built up since the last bathing opportunity, usually a week to ten days before. The end result was smooth, clean, soft, and lightly scented skin. Between their trips to the baths, people simply did the best they could to keep clean by using water and cloth, or, if they were fortunate, a natural sponge and some warm water, if and when they were fortunate enough to have warm water.

Longinus and Julius were surprised at how warm—no, make that *hot*—the water bubbling out of the natural rock pool was; so hot that it was difficult to get into the first pool. When people had been in it for a few minutes, their skin began to turn red. Most people couldn't stay very long before they wanted the relief and refreshment of a cooler pool

The hot water felt good on Longinus's wounded arm. Perhaps there was some kind of special healing in these outdoor pools, he thought. His head wound was fine now; only a thin red scar remained on his forehead where the helmet had left its mark. *Better a scar than if I had been without the helmet,* he mused. *And the scar is also a mark of valor.*

He remembered with a wince how the physician had removed the sutures from his arm. First, the doctor straightened one end of a wire suture. Next, he had washed the area with some wine and then quickly and deftly plucked the suture out by pulling on the other end. Longinus had felt a stinging, burning sensation as the doctor removed the wires, but the pain was soon gone, and the tissue had since healed. Now a red-pink scar remained where there had been a jagged gash.

"Just be sure not to lift anything heavy with that arm, soldier," the doctor had warned Longinus. "The bones are healing, but you need to give them time to gain back strength. Then you'll be as fit as ever. You are a lucky man to have survived with only the injuries you have."

It hardly seemed possible to Longinus that he had looked death in the eye only forty days before, and now he was here, smiling and enjoying the Roman baths. He had made a commitment to himself just after his brush with death. He vowed to enjoy every day and every minute of life. His near-death experience had somehow energized him. Every color seemed more vivid; every experience more profound. He intended to make the most of life, whatever it would bring. The sixty-day paid leave, the eagle signet ring, and the silver reward were definitely a good start on his vow.

He'd been in the army two and a half years already. He found it to be challenging as well as rewarding. Most of all, he had experienced the acceptance, recognition, and upward mobility he had so desperately longed for when he was working in his father's leather shop. He felt he had found what he needed to fill his soul—almost. However, there was still an elusive emptiness that had yet to be filled. He couldn't define it, but it lurked just below the surface, like the pebbles in the pool. Occasionally, that emptiness bubbled to the surface, disturbing his inner tranquility.

For the moment, though, he ignored the tug of that void and gratefully soaked up the rest and relaxation of the immediate experience. The water, the blue sky, and the warm sun, as well as the absence of the marching, drilling, and especially of the cacophony of battle—all combined to bring true relaxation.

Here, the toast-your-skin-brown warmth of the sun, the bubbling, healing artesian water, and the cloudless sky saturated his senses with pure pleasure. He could just close his eyes and allow himself to drift in the delight of the soothingly warm water.

In his reverie, Longinus became vaguely aware of the sound of galloping hoofs. *A horse and rider must be nearby. Unusual,* he thought, *only military commanders or the very wealthy have the means to buy and maintain those magnificent animals.*

He opened his eyes slowly, raising his hand to shield them from the sun's polished-brass brightness. The horse was the sleekest, best-groomed animal he had ever seen. It was a rich, warm brown, like the patina that forms on high-quality bronze. He was captivated by its graceful beauty. The steed moved swiftly, smoothly, and powerfully, its muscles rippling under its shiny coat—giving the appearance of only lightly touching the earth as it glided along.

Maybe, Longinus fantasized, *when I become a centurion, I can own such a beautiful mount.* He had daydreamed of such a time. All eyes would turn to him with admiration. He determined that he would be in that position someday. He would do well in the legions and work his way up. His plan was to stay in the legions as long as he could—he was in this for a career. The military had become his life, his family, and his identity. In his imagination, he saw himself in command of a large number of troops. All of his men would respond quickly and capably to his able and professional leadership. There would be no limit to what he could do, where he could go, or what he could become. The reverie brought a smile to his face and hope to his heart.

Then Longinus shifted his focus to the rider. If the mount had captivated him, he was *awestruck* by the rider. She was a young woman, and she rode easily, with an air of command, control, and confidence the likes of which he had never seen before. Her long, red-bronze hair flowed freely behind her as the wind swept past her lovely face.

Her face—he couldn't take his eyes off her face. Her clear, smooth features were as finely chiseled as any cameo he had ever seen. Her sparkling green eyes made the forest look dull by comparison. She was regal. Beautiful. Stunning.

She was also absolutely unaware of his wide-eyed, slack-jawed admiration.

Time stood still for Longinus. Everything went into slow motion, much as it had when the barbarian nearly killed him. The difference was that while his heart had frozen in fear when the barbarian had confronted him, now his heart nearly stopped beating as, in absolute awe, he watched the elegant rider as she galloped by.

He willed himself to drink in every detail, as a desert-sun-parched man would drink in cool water, savoring every molecule of the life-giving liquid. Liquid! Yes, liquid! That's how she moved. Every movement was fluid. Easy. Smooth. Like a fluid—flowing, flooding, and inundating his emotions and senses as she rode past.

"Longinus! Breathe, man—breathe, or you'll pass out!" Julius said, laughing as he playfully elbowed his friend. Longinus then realized that he had indeed been holding his breath—as if, should he stop breathing, by some magic she would cease galloping by and become suspended in midair so he could continue to drink in her beauty.

"That's very unusual," observed Julius, "a young woman riding alone like that. She seems very sure of herself."

"Uh-huh," Longinus mumbled. "I wonder who she is?"

"Who knows?" responded Julius. "But that was a vision of true beauty, my friend."

"You're certainly right there, Julius," said Longinus. "You are absolutely right. I have never seen someone so beautiful. I do wonder who she is. Aren't you curious too?"

"Of course, but your interest goes beyond curiosity."

Longinus felt his face flush a bright red—and it wasn't because of the temperature of the pool. He'd seen attractive young women before. But, because soldiers were not officially allowed to marry—and the key word here is *officially*—he hadn't allowed himself to take much interest before this.

Many soldiers did marry, of course, but their marriages weren't deemed official until they retired from the legions after twenty or more years of service. At retirement, soldiers were given an official bronze tablet, or *diploma*. That document both recognized their service to Rome and validated their family, legitimizing their children and bestowing Roman citizenship on them as well. The *diploma* was one of the most valued and valuable items any soldier could ever hope to have. With it came also a parcel of land and a retirement stipend. Of course, the greater the rank, the greater the rewards a retiree would receive.

Because the *diploma* wasn't granted until the soldier completed military service, families tended to stay together up through retirement. While the soldier stayed in the barracks—for official functions and accountability—the family would live in the temporary communities that followed the troops wherever they went, except, of course, into battle.

Marriage? Retirement? What was Longinus thinking? These events would be a long way down the road. He was "married" to his chosen profession of soldiering in the legions. And he intended to put every ounce of energy he had into *that* relationship and *that* career. He had decided that's where he would find his fulfillment. He was in love with his work and with the challenges and camaraderie that came with being a soldier. To him, enlisting was the best decision he had ever made.

Maybe someday he'd marry. But maybe not. His own home life hadn't been that fulfilling. His father had ruled the family with the proverbial iron fist. His own home and his personal experiences there didn't recommend marriage to him. *Better to be single and free,* he thought.

After all, it was his friend Julius, basking in the pool next to him, who had saved his life only a few weeks before. And their mutual valor had saved the life of their commander, Pontius Pilate, and earned them both a handsome reward, including this idyllic break from the daily rigors of the military life. Could a mere wife do that? Would a wife risk her life for him against a brutish barbarian, as Julius had done? No, the military was his life—his love. That was enough, for now.

But that rider really was beautiful. He wondered if she might ride by again tomorrow. He fervently hoped so. After all, just because you didn't intend to climb a mountain didn't mean that you couldn't enjoy looking at the scenery.

Longinus eased back into the hot water, closed his eyes, and in his mind watched as she rode by again and again and again. His smile deepened with each succeeding vision.

The next day, Longinus decided to go on a long walk to build up his endurance so that when he went back to his unit, he would be fit and could keep up with all the marching and drills. As he walked briskly along a dirt path, he heard a horse galloping toward him from behind. Knowing that the horse might shy if he stood too close to the path, he stepped aside and waited for the horse and rider to pass. As he did, his heart leaped with the possibility that it might be the same rider as he had seen the day before. At least he could hope so.

Then, there she was—the same young woman on the same horse. She would pass right by him. He searched frantically for a way to initiate conversation with her, though he knew by the way she was riding that she had no intention of stopping for him or anyone else.

As she passed, she turned and gave him a courteous nod to thank him for stepping off the path. A slight smile came to her face. Longinus thought his knees might buckle as she galloped by.

Then he saw it. A scroll had fallen from her saddlebag. He watched as it tumbled to the ground, rolled, and then stopped. She rode on, unaware of the loss.

Longinus ran to scoop up the scroll. He had a fleeting hope that he might get her attention and give it back to her, but by the time he had retrieved it, she had turned a corner and was gone.

He stood there, scroll in hand, wondering what to do next. He had no idea where she was headed, and there was no way he could catch up with her.

Longinus looked down at the fine leather parchment tied with a blue ribbon. His curiosity got the best of him, and he untied the ribbon to see what she might have been reading. As he did, a slight, sweet scent wafted from the scroll.

The scroll contained a lengthy list of names, dates, and funds due. It was some kind of accounting record—of what, he had no idea, but obviously, it was of value to someone. What could he do?

An idea struck him. The girl had ridden by at about the same time twice now. Perhaps she would come this way tomorrow too. He'd be there if she did.

The next day, Longinus picked an open spot where he would see her coming at quite a distance, and she would also be able to see him. The openness of the place had an additional advantage. She might feel threatened and probably wouldn't stop in some secluded place. He could hardly blame her for that.

About the time he thought that she might ride by again, he heard the sound of hoof beats. Sure enough, it was her! This time, she was riding more slowly and looking down at the path as she rode. It was clear to Longinus that she was looking for the scroll he held in his hand.

He stood up, walked to the middle of the path, held up the scroll, and began to wave it gently back and forth, both to catch her attention and to let her know he had the scroll. It took a while for her to notice him, but then she saw him waving the scroll. At that, she quickened the pace of her horse and rode directly to Longinus with a look of relief on her face.

"I think this is what you're looking for," he said, holding out the scroll.

"Yes, it is, sir. I lost it yesterday and have been frantic to find it."

"I saw it fall from your saddlebag yesterday, but couldn't get your attention in time to return it to you," he said, reaching it toward her. "Here! It's my pleasure to return it to you."

She took the scroll, opened it, and smiled broadly. "Yes, this is it!" she exclaimed with a smile.

Longinus looked intently at the intelligent green eyes of the beautiful woman on the horse. She was even more stunning close up.

"What's your name?" she asked.

"I am Longinus," he replied, hoping to open a long conversation with her.

"Thank you for your kindness, Longinus," she said. Then she galloped off, leaving Longinus standing on the path, greatly disappointed.

"Well," he said to himself, "at least I got close enough to her to get more than a glimpse this time. That's something, anyhow."

Then he walked back to Saalburg with a smile on his face. It had been a good afternoon.

Questions for Thought and Discussion

1. The Roman bath pools ranged from hot (*caldarium*) to warm (*tepidarium*) to cold (*frigidarium*). Where, along that same continuum, would you rate your spiritual life to be right now? Where would you like it to be? What will you do to move from where you are on the scale? How can you help others move on the scale?

2. The Roman *strigil* was used to scrape away the dirt and dead skin, and oils were used to restore and relax the skin. What scrapes away your "deadness"? What restores and relaxes you?

3. What has God used as His *strigil* to clean up your life? What was the process like? What was the end result?

4. For a Roman soldier, the *diploma* was the ultimate recognition of who he was and what he had accomplished. What is your equivalent—your *diploma*?

5. Remember, reflect, and recount your first encounter with that special person in your life. What was it like? What initially attracted you? How did the relationship develop? What are you doing now to keep that relationship vibrant, new, and exciting?

6. Longinus was aware of an emptiness—a void—in his life. What do you think was lacking for him? What has made your life fulfilling? What might be lacking right now?

Chapter 5

REFLECTIONS

Only twenty days of leisure at the fort and spa remained for Longinus and Julius, and then it would be back to marching, drills, and battle lines again. The break was good, but Longinus missed being with his unit. The bonds formed while in the legions were unique and hard to explain to someone who had never experienced them. The daily training, work, and weapons maintenance became threads in a broad and strong fabric of friendship that was unlike anything Longinus had previously experienced. One's life depended on one's friends. More than mere friendship, more than family, this bond developed into a committed loyalty on which each soldier would and did stake his life.

The downtime in Saalburg gave Longinus time to look back to where he had been and where he wanted to go with his life. His own father hadn't been much of a role model. Even though a few years had passed now, his father's parting words—disowning and rejecting him—still felt like salt in a wound. He didn't hate his father, but he surely didn't want to become a copy of him either. Probably, the old man was doing the best he could with his limited education and day-to-day, hand-to-mouth existence.

And that's all it had been—mere existence. Longinus had left home because he wanted a deep connection, and he wanted to see the world, to expand his experience, and to be somebody. He knew he couldn't find that in the tiny village where he grew up. *But now,* he thought, *I've finally found the key to what I've been looking for.* He smiled to himself as he recalled the first days of legionary life, which were still indelibly etched in his mind. . . .

When he had arrived at the fort where he was to receive his initial military training, he was met by the grizzled older soldier Aquinas Marius, who bore the auspicious title, "master at arms." His job was to train the new recruits, an assignment so important to the legions that he and other masters at arms were also known as a *duplicarii*—soldiers who drew double pay.

Aquinas had immediately harangued his ten new recruits—who were more scared than they would admit. "So, you children want to be Roman soldiers, huh? We'll see about that. My job is to see to it that you have what it takes to be in *my* legion. To see if you have what it takes to protect *my* life. To find out if you are fit to be in *my* unit. For the next two months, I'll be your father, your mother, and your god. What I say, you'll do without any question, backtalk, or whining. I don't put up with whiners, so if you get tired or sore or hurt, just tough it out.

"One more thing," he had said, as he raised a polished, reddish-brown, knot-covered swagger stick. "This friend of mine is called a *vitis*. It's made from a grapevine. It's tough and resilient, just like I'm going to make you. If you get out of line or if you whine, I'm going to wallop you with it."

The *vitis* was a stout, grapevine "swagger stick" that centurions and others carried as a symbol of authority. It was frequently used as an "attitude adjuster."

Longinus had looked at the stick. It was about five handbreadths long, and he could see where branches had been. In most places, they had left hard, raised knobs. The *vitis* ended in a tightly curled burl that could easily pass for a small but tough clenched fist. It would create an instant knot on the hapless trainee who would be disciplined by it. That was instantly clear.

As if reading their minds, Aquinas had barked, "If you're too slow to respond, my *vitis* will tattoo a lump on your hide to help you along, speed you up, or help you remember what I say. Now, *run* to supply and draw your clothes and equipment. *Run,* I said—RUN!"

Some hesitation ensued, because even though the recruits all knew how to run, they didn't know which way to go. Aquinas had solved that conundrum by soundly thumping the nearest recruit—who happened to be Longinus—on the back with the *vitis* and then pointing the way with that instrument of torture. The recruits all ran like rabbits being chased by a fox, while Aquinas yelled, "Run! Move, you bunch of prissy little women. Move, maggots! Run!"

At that point, Longinus questioned whether he'd made the right decision to leave home and join the legions. But it hadn't mattered then—he couldn't quit. Besides, his pride and his father's parting words wouldn't let him go back home. There was only one thing to do: run—and that he could do. A welt was rising on his back, but he didn't say a word. He'd rather die than brand himself a sissy.

When they got to the issue point, they saw racks of armor, piles of sandals, and stacks of garments. There was far more clothing than Longinus had ever seen in one place. Most Roman families were lucky to have two garments each.

"Don't just stand there and gawk. Move up to the table," the recruits' new father-mother-god barked to those at the front of the line. And before the fellow in front could respond, the *vitis* whistled through the air and caught him in the middle of the back. The blow propelled him to the table, gasping for breath. A young soldier behind the table threw the recruit two tunics. They were worn and patched. The design was simple. Basically, the tunic consisted of two pieces of lightweight wool stitched together into what could have been a sack with two arm holes and another hole for the head.

"Strip down and dump all your civilian clothes in a pile right here," Aquinas ordered, gesturing to a spot at his feet. "You aren't going to need anything but what the legion supplies. Oh—and it isn't free. You'll pay us back. We'll take it out of your salary, so take care of it or you'll go broke pretty quickly."

"You mean we have to change our good stuff for these . . . these rags?" Pulcher had protested.

Aquinas had squinted at him and hissed, "These 'rags' will be plenty good enough for the likes of you, rat-face. If you make it through my training, you'll have more proper attire, but you have to earn that right. We aren't giving you good stuff now. You don't deserve it. You're only *probatio,* you know—you're on probation until you can prove to me that you are good enough to be a soldier. So pick up what is issued to you, open your ears, and shut your mouth."

Pulcher shot back, "I'm going to fold up my stuff and keep it. No point in dumping it on the ground."

Quicker than the blink of an eye, Aquinas's *vitis* whistled through the air and caught Pulcher on the side of the head, knocking him out like a candle in a gale.

"OK," barked Aquinas. "You've just seen lesson number one and lesson number two."

The recruits knew instinctively not to ask what the lessons were, but they really wanted to know. It didn't take long for them to find out.

"First, when I tell you to do something, do it—and do it quickly." Aquinas bit off each word slowly and distinctly as he said it, making an indelible impression on the remaining *probatio* trembling before him.

"Second, no backtalk and no comments. When I give an order, ladies, it's an order—not a suggestion or an invitation. Do you understand?"

The wide-eyed recruits wordlessly nodded yes. They understood very clearly. No more demonstrations were needed. They got it.

"When hardhead here wakes up, help him with those lessons," Aquinas said. "You teach him. That's your responsibility. You're gonna teach each other to work, to fight, and to survive together. Do you get it?"

The nine recruits still standing nodded to indicate that they absolutely got the message.

Reminiscing, Longinus had to smile at the experiences of the past. He recalled the incessant drills, the marching, the spear throwing, and the sword and shield drills. He had listened, and he had learned. Something else had happened too. He had both toughened up and bulked up. He'd been as skinny as a wheel spoke when he joined the legion. Now, he was solidly muscular and catlike quick. Others who had tended to the other extreme—"lard-fat momma's boys," as Aquinas called them—lost weight and were quite fit now too.

Best of all, Longinus learned to listen, to observe, and to anticipate orders even before Aquinas barked them out.

Some of the trainees called Aquinas their "tor-mentor." He was every bit as tough as his *vitis*. But he was also fair and thorough. There were no "pet" trainees, nor was there a goat. He trained them all, disciplined them all, and pushed them all to do more than they ever thought they could.

One day, unexpectedly, Aquinas had called Longinus aside. "I've been watching you closely," he said.

"Sir, yes sir. Is there a problem, sir? If so, I'll work on it, sir."

"No," responded Aquinas. "Quite the contrary. I like what I see in you. You have what it takes to be a soldier. More than that, you have what it takes to be a leader of soldiers."

All Longinus could do was to blink and blush at what he heard. He finally managed to stammer, "Thank you, sir—I don't know what to say."

"Nothing to say. Just keep the positive attitude you have now, and you'll make a real name for yourself.

"One more thing," Aquinas continued. "Learn to do what is right from the core of your being. That's what success and soldiering is all about."

"Right? How will I know what—?"

Aquinas cut in. "Listen to your heart. Pay attention to the essence of who you are. Trust what you hear there, and you'll know what is right. Now, go back to those sword drills."

Longinus kept running that phrase through his mind: *"Learn to do what's right from the core of your being."* He resolved that he would live that way—that he would listen to his core; that he would make a name for himself; that he would, as Aquinas said, be a "leader of others." Longinus knew that the rough-and-ready trainer had given him a gift. He could see that the advice was a key to unlock deeper realities and potentials—a compass that could orient his every experience.

Aquinas wasn't short on experience. He had enough battle scars on his body and enough years in the legions to speak with authority. He'd "been there; done that" many times over, and he was willing to share what he knew with the *probatio*. While he was as tough as his *vitis,* there was a unique depth to him as well.

"Learn to do what is right. . . . Listen to your heart. . . . Pay attention to your inner core. . . ." Longinus repeated the words and weighed them like gold coins. He resolved to make them part of his life, his ethics, and his practice.

The Centurion

The recruit training was rigorous. Their time was divided among the various skills they were required to master. For instance, they had to learn to swim well. Longinus was a good swimmer, and to his credit, he taught some of the others the skill, thus fulfilling Aquinas's statement that they should and would teach each other.

One of the toughest parts of training involved working with the wicker double-weight shield—the *cratis*—and the double-weight wooden practice sword known as the *clava.* Both instruments were used for extensive drill and practice twice per day. Sometimes the trainees would charge, stab, and slash at a six-foot upright pole planted firmly in the ground to simulate an enemy soldier. The post was called a *palus.* In one area were multiple poles, *pali,* to represent multiple antagonists. Aquinas roared at the trainees to "Stab! Stab! Don't slash when you go for the body. A slash will only wound. A two-inch stab is fatal. So, stab with your sword. Harder! Faster!"

At other times, they were to drill with each other. That proved to be a bruising experience. The idea was to use the double-weight shield as a battering ram to knock your opponent off balance and then use the sword to finish him off. It was during one of these encounters that Pulcher had nearly killed Longinus—or so Longinus thought.

Using the double-weight instruments was exhausting, but the aim was to build up the soldiers' strength and endurance. When they were issued the real equipment—actually, when they were allowed to purchase it—it would feel so light that they'd feel confident using it.

Some days, the training included the use of spears. They would throw them at the posts that represented the enemy. The practice spears also were extra heavy and took enormous effort to throw. On other days, the trainees were taught the use of the bow and battle arrows, even though most of them would be infantrymen, not archers. They all had to become efficient enough with a bow to hit a bundle of reeds from six hundred feet away. Those deemed to have good skills with the bow were later given additional training and drafted into the ranks of the archers.

Another skill required the use of a sling made of two long pieces of cord with a leather pouch in the middle. Slings were easy to carry, light, and quite effective. The rocks they propelled and the lead "bullets"—called *glandes* because they were cast in the shape of a double-pointed acorn—could be deadly up to fifteen hundred feet, more than double the effective range of an arrow. Aquinas told them that the lead projectiles were especially deadly because they were so small that the enemy couldn't see them coming. "You can see an arrow coming at you from a distance because of its size," he said. "The *glans* is small enough and dark enough to be practically invisible, and it's heavy enough to kill or wound the enemy before they know it's on the way. And if you run out of the lead pieces, you can always use rocks." The idea was to make each recruit skillful in using a wide range of weapons beyond the basic shield, sword, and spear.

After several weeks of training, Aquinas showed up with a handful of small metal discs on leather cords. By this time, several of the trainees had either dropped out or been deemed unworthy to continue and sent home. "This is a transition for you," Aquinas commented. "You have come far enough that I believe you will soon be soldiers, not trainees. Therefore, my gift to each of you is a *signaculum.* It has your name and our unit identification engraved on it. Wear it around your neck at all times. It's your identity—who you are, and whose you are."

So the training continued. Longinus learned to carry the sixty pounds of field pack and armor on twenty-five-mile-long marches. At first, he thought he would die of exhaustion, but he encouraged his friends, and they encouraged him, and ultimately, they all made it. As the training went on, they became better accustomed to the marches, and although these were never fun, they became less difficult as the trainees became more physically fit and supportive of each other.

One of the last things they had to learn was how to build a temporary fortress in the field by digging a nine-foot-wide, seven-foot-deep trench around their perimeter. They used the excavated dirt to build an earthen wall, which they studded with palisade stakes (*pila muralia*)—five-foot-tall, double-pointed wood pieces that could be implanted in the ground and tied together to form a picket fence at the top of the earthen wall. Or the stakes could be lashed together in threes to form spiky obstacles studded with spearlike points. These formidable obstacles were placed in the ditch, making it difficult for the enemy to thread their way through and into the fort.

Each trainee was issued one or two of the *pila muralia* to add to his already heavy marching pack. At first, Longinus saw them only as extra weight—

"another dumb piece of dead weight to pack around." But when he saw how his pieces, combined with those of his fellows, could protect them all, he was impressed with both the obstacles and the concept of teamwork they represented.

At first, Longinus had feared Aquinas, but as the training went on, he began to respect him and the craft of soldiering he obviously knew so well. And Longinus reflected even more deeply on what Aquinas had shared with him: *"Learn to do what is right. Listen to your heart. Pay attention to your inner core."* Longinus determined that he would live by those sayings. He would be a superior soldier. He would serve the emperor with absolute fidelity.

Now, as he lounged in the warm, soothing waters of the pool on his paid leave, the days when he was a trainee seemed to be in the distant past.

Well, he thought, *soon enough we'll be back in the legion again, and this experience will be only a memory.* With a smile of determination to enjoy every remaining moment of his free time, Longinus slipped deeper into the relaxing waters.

Questions for Thought and Discussion

1. Longinus left home because he was seeking to expand his experiences. How do you seek to expand your experiences? What part does spirituality and faith play in that process?

2. What have you learned from someone you would regard as your personal Aquinas? Who was or is that person? What life sayings serve as mission statements or guides for your life and decisions? From whom did you gain those mottos?

3. Roman basic training was meant to instill a sense of teamwork and unity. Does that philosophy prevail in your home, your workplace or school, or your congregation? What parts of that philosophy are most important to you?

4. The new Roman recruits (*probatio*) had to wear a *signaculum*—the equivalent of modern dog tags—for identification purposes. What identifies who you are? What identifies *whose* you are?

5. Roman soldiers were cross-trained with various kinds of weapons and skills so they could function well in a wide variety of circumstances.

What are some of the spiritual weapons you are using on your own behalf and for the good of those around you? What spiritual weapons might you need to add to that arsenal?

6. Reflect on some change points and people who have shaped your life and helped you become who you are today. Who is your mentor right now? If you do not have a mentor, who will you invite to be your mentor? When and how will you do it? Whom are you mentoring?

Chapter 6

NEW HORIZONS

When Longinus and Julius began their leave, they slept late in the mornings and spent most of the rest of their days lounging around and in the pools. But in time, they started to become bored with this routine—if it could even be called a routine. They also thought about all the drilling and marching they'd be doing when they rejoined their unit. They knew that if they let themselves become unfit while on leave, they'd be sorry when they returned to regular duty. So they began to do increasingly lengthy marches through the country-side, challenging each other as to how far they could go and how quickly they could cover the courses they set for themselves. They enjoyed these workouts, and the pools were even more inviting after they had exerted themselves.

On one of their long marches near the end of their leave, their conversation lagged. Over the past few weeks, they had covered just about every subject of interest to them, so for a while they were lost in their own thoughts. Longinus's mind drifted back to the day when Aquinas deemed that his recruits were ready to be transferred into regular soldiering positions in the legion.

Besides subduing outlying regions and maintaining control in the empire, the Roman army was tasked with fabricating roads, buildings, ports, and other parts of the infrastructure of value to the emperor. So in addition to soldiering and combat skills, all soldiers, including Longinus and Julius, were taught a variety of building and engineering trades. These included how to survey land, how to cut and lay stone, and how to build roads that would last for centuries.

Of course, the "good jobs" were highly coveted and hard to get. Longinus and Julius were posted to the stone quarry. It wasn't the most desirable assignment, but it was a relief from Aquinas's incessant drilling and general harassment. While their trainer had assured them he was pushing them to their limits only to expand those limits so they would be ready to deal with battle, they all longed for the day when they would be out of the reach of his tongue and *vitis*. In unit assignments, they would have a more regular schedule, more choices, and more of the spare time they coveted.

One good thing, Longinus had reflected, *is that Publius Pulcher is assigned to another part of the legion.* Apparently, Pulcher had some past experience with horses, so he was sent to an equestrian unit. Not that Pulcher would actually ever own a horse. In fact, he might never be allowed to ride one. Longinus had smiled as he pictured Pulcher ankle-deep in the stables, shoveling them clean. *I'd rather be here making big rocks into little rocks in the quarry and working outdoors than stuffed away in some stinky stable. And this way, I don't have to work with that pain of a person,* he had thought as he rubbed the ribs that Pulcher had injured several weeks before during their training.

Stonecutting was indeed hard work, but as Longinus and Julius worked with the senior stonecutters, they quickly learned how to cut and shape stone. Longinus and Julius not only deepened their friendship with each other but learned a great deal about engineering, tools, teamwork, and planning. They soon learned to look ahead several steps in the stonecutting process. By making plans on where to split the rock and how to do that, they learned that having a plan made a world of difference in how much work was done, how efficiently tasks were completed.

Not long after starting work in the quarry, one of Longinus's sandals broke. That night he did a quick repair, using skills he'd learned in his father's leather shop, where he'd made hundreds of sandals in various shapes, designs, and styles. A few days later, one of Julius's sandals failed too, so Longinus did that repair as well. His skills in working with leather and with people did not go unnoticed. One morning, Mario, the *optio,* or second-in-charge of the century, ordered Longinus to report to the centurion's command room. Surprised by the summons, Longinus wondered what he might have done wrong. He racked his brain, wondering what the problem might be.

Caligae were boots or sandals with hobnail soles that provided grip, prevented wear, and in battle, made soldiers' kicks more damaging.

When Mario ushered Longinus into the commander's chambers, Longinus's face betrayed his inner concerns. He felt as if he had been summoned to some great punishment and was just waiting for the sentence to be pronounced. Afraid? No, he wasn't just afraid—he was terrified.

"Legionnaire Longinus, sir," barked the *optio,* as he pushed Longinus into the formidable presence of the centurion, Quintus.

"Longinus—that is Greek for *spear* or *lance,* isn't it, son?" observed Quintus from behind his massive oak and leather desk. Longinus could see that the desk was both portable and beautifully made, with polished wood legs, drawers that held maps and other materials, and a finely carved leather top. The leather, of course, caught his attention. But he dared not stare, so he looked at the wall behind the commander as he stood fencepost-straight at attention.

"Yes, sir," he responded, bringing his closed right fist to the center of his chest in a smart salute. "My name does mean 'the spear.' "

"Relax, son," said Quintus. "I just wanted to meet you personally and ask about your skills. My *optio* here says that you are excellent with leatherwork. He tells me that you also have a good way of working with soldiers too."

Then Mario smiled at Longinus and said, "You can breathe easy. You seemed worried when you entered the room."

"Well, sir—sirs—I didn't know what to expect. I've been trying my hardest to learn and to be a productive part of the unit, but—"

"So, Longinus," the centurion interrupted, "how did you become acquainted with leatherwork?"

"Before I came into the legions, sir, I worked with my father in his leather shop. I've been working with leather since I was old enough to hold an awl."

Longinus told the commander, as he had Julius, about his experiences in his father's shop, and how working with leather and sandals was second nature to him.

"Very interesting," Quintus said, smiling. "How would you like to change from the quarry to the leather shop in the *fabrica* as your assignment in the legion?"

Before Longinus could respond, the *optio* interjected, "Being in the leather shop is an exempt assignment, Longinus. An *immunis*. Do you know what that means?"

"Exempt?" Longinus's puzzlement was obvious.

The centurion laughed and explained, "An *immunis* assignment means that you will be excused from the routine rotational duty roster. No guard duty, no kitchen duty, no latrine duty, and no camp clean-up details. You'll still be required to do your regular training with your gladius, spear, shield, and other gear. You'll still march with the unit when we go to the field. You'll still be required to be 'fit to fight' and ready to do so if there is a need, but you will be exempt from the other duties. How does that sound to you?"

Longinus responded quickly. "Sir, that sounds fine with me. Just fine! Great! If that is where you want me to serve, I'll be glad to work in the leather shop. Yes, sir—just fine!"

"In that case, consider it done. I will issue orders assigning you there beginning in the morning," promised the commander. "Report there right after the morning sword drill. They'll be expecting you. See to the orders, *optio*."

With that, Longinus and Mario were dismissed, and Longinus was released to go back to his quarters.

It's ironic, Longinus had thought to himself as he walked back to the barracks. He had joined the legions precisely to get *away* from working with his father in the leather shop. Now, he was delighted to be working with leather again. He just smiled and shook his head. *Life is strange!*

He had been so absorbed in thought that he nearly ran into Julius, who was coming around a tent from another direction.

"Longinus, you won't believe what happened to me just now!" Julius said excitedly.

"What?" inquired Longinus. "You've been selected to be a member of the Roman senate?"

Julius laughed heartily. "Not quite that good, but pretty close. I've been selected to work in the armory. I will be trained as a *custos armorum*—an armorer. The legion is developing a new type of armor, and I get to be part of the process."

Longinus fell into step with Julius as they headed toward their tent. They had become so used to marching that they automatically fell into a marching cadence. Longinus shared his good fortune at being selected to work in the leather shop. Both assignments were exempt, and both would take them away from the hot, hard work in the quarry.

Even though they worked in different parts of the camp, they continued to stay in the same barracks. And their friendship grew and deepened as they adapted to the military routine and continued to hone their military skills. Beyond that, they learned to trust and work with other soldiers in the unit. Pride in the unit, trust, and loyalty became the watchwords of their lives. The words of Aquinas kept coming back to Longinus: *"Go with your heart. Go with your heart."* Was this what Aquinas meant? Was working together with others in the unit, developing friendships, and building unity part of following your heart? Perhaps so.

The sense of belonging that Longinus experienced was unlike anything he had felt before. The legion gave him a sense of purpose, a sense of belonging, and a sense of meaning and accomplishment. Even the routine work and sword drill added to the connection he felt with his fellow legionnaires.

This sense of belonging had prompted a discussion with Julius and several of the others in the barracks about doing something that would make their unit distinctive and unique. Oh, sure, the legion had its identifying design on their shields and on the *vexillum*—a flag the units used while operating away from the main legionary force. All the units had those. "What could we do to leave a mark—a real mark—so everyone will know that our unit has been there?" Marcellus, one of their barrack mates had asked.

"Leave a mark . . . Leave a mark . . . Hmmm," mused Longinus, half to himself and half to the others.

The next night, as the group sat around the fire, Longinus reached into his leather bag and pulled out a sandal he had made in the shop earlier in the day. "This, my friends, is how we can leave our mark," he said as he held up the sandal. "Wherever we go, people will know we've been there."

"What's special about that? It's just a military sandal," observed one of the soldiers.

"Take a closer look," encouraged Longinus as he tossed the sandal to the man. "I'll give you a clue," he continued. "Look at the sole."

All Roman sandals had hobnails that held the leather sole to the rest of the sandal and prevented excessive wear of the sole.

"I'm not sure what I'm supposed to see here," the curious soldier said.

"Look again," encouraged Longinus. "Use a little imagination."

"It looks like a stick figure of a man."

"So far, so good. What is the man doing?"

"His legs are bent like—as if he's kneeling," responded the soldier.

"You are absolutely right," Longinus said as he excitedly took the sandal from the man's hand and held it up for the others to see.

"I arranged the nails in a new pattern. It pictures a man kneeling. He's begging for mercy. It's our message to any and all. It tells them, 'You want mercy from me? There will be no mercy. If you aren't a Roman, we will walk on you; so fall in line with us or you will have our footprints all over your body.' "

"And," continued Longinus, "even after we leave an area, we will have left an imprint of our unit, of our legion, and of Rome itself. Our sandals have all sorts of designs on them. Why not have a design that makes a real statement?"

"Impressive," commented Marcellus as he turned the sandal over in his large, rough hands. Others who had gathered around the flickering light to see the new design murmured their agreement.

"But couldn't it create problems for us?" asked one of the soldiers, "I mean, it's hardly an invitation for the locals to be our friends."

"True enough," said Longinus, pausing for dramatic effect. "But the message is for the uncultured rabble we have to subdue for Rome. It will work on their heads," he said, tapping his forehead with his fingers. "They'll develop a healthy fear of us—respect for us—or they will feel the crushing blow of Rome on their bodies. They get to choose either to cooperate with us and have these prints on their soil, or not to cooperate with us and have these prints on their backs."

A ripple of enthusiastic agreement swept through the group. They nodded and smiled their approval.

"It's a great idea!" shouted one of the soldiers.

"Show it to the *optio*," said another.

"All right, I will," responded a smiling Longinus. "I'll show it to him in the morning. No, better yet, I'll give these new sandals to the *optio* so he can see the design and try out the sandals."

"I'll come with you," Julius spoke up. "I've been wearing the sandals you made for me for several months now. I can tell him how much more comfortable they are than some of the old patterns we've had in the past. The new nail pattern will convince him that this is what we need for our unit!"

"We'll go together then," said Longinus.

The next morning, Mario, the *optio,* had been wary at first. It was quite bold for these two new troops to begin making suggestions about changes in the unit. But they were bold but not cocky, he had observed. They were creative, enthusiastic, and willing to change—all marks of potential leaders.

As he examined the sandals, he immediately saw the careful craftsmanship and attention to detail. And the young men wanted to make a statement for Rome. These were all good traits—traits of solid soldiers and potential leaders in the legion. Mario was impressed with their initiative and creativity.

He agreed to wear the new sandals for a few weeks before he made a decision, especially before broaching the subject to the centurion, Quintus. After all, part of his job as *optio* was to filter out the "ash and trash" before the boss had to deal with it.

After a few days, Mario had to admit that this new style of sandal *was* more comfortable than what he had worn before—something about how it laced and fit. He also took note that others were noticing the pattern the hobnails made in the dirt as he strode by. Clearly, the nails were leaving an impression on those who saw the imprint—an impression on people as well as in the dirt. *Yes,* Mario had reflected, *this Longinus may really have what it takes to be a good soldier, maybe even a leader. I'll keep a close eye on him.*

The summer day was hot, and Longinus could feel the sweat trickling down his back as he worked in the leather *fabrica*. Today, he was cutting leather strips for the new kind of armor Julius and his friends were working on. The current interlocking ring armor was heavy. Worse than that, it chafed the skin, leaving the wearer really uncomfortable by the end of the day. Julius claimed that the new, banded *lorica* was both more comfortable and lighter than the old armor. That was welcome news to anyone who had to wear armor most of the day or on a long march. A more serious drawback of the armor they had been using was that a strongly thrown *pila* could split the rings, offering the wearer no protection. Julius claimed that the new armor would more readily deflect a spear or arrow.

Pila muralia could be lashed together to form a line of defense difficult for enemy troops to penetrate.

The leather shop was in the far corner of the camp, against the outer wall. Some days the rock wall kept the room cool. But when the sun beat down on the rock, it seemed to hold and radiate heat all day. And, of course, the wall also cut off any breeze. This was one of those hot afternoons.

Longinus was so intent on his work that he didn't see Mario enter the shop. Only when he noticed that the chatter and hammering had stopped did he look up. Mario was standing in front of him. Startled, Longinus immediately came to attention. "Sir—Legionnaire Longinus, sir," he said automatically.

"Come with me now," said Mario.

This abrupt command was unnerving. The eyes of the rest of the leatherworking crew opened wide at the command. Then Longinus relaxed as he saw Mario break into a broad grin. "These sandals are the best I've ever worn in my twenty years in the legions," Mario said. "That, and the comments I've had about the nail-print sole patterns, have convinced me that we need to take this idea of yours to the centurion. I like your idea of using this design for our cohort. It will make us distinctive."

Longinus grinned from ear to ear. "You like them that much?"

"Sure do. Clean up a bit, and let's go. The centurion is expecting us. Bring a sample sandal and a copy of the nail pattern with you."

"Well, sir, in fact, I have a pair of sandals that I made to fit the centurion. I'm not trying to be presumptuous, but I try to be prepared. I took the measurements of his foot when he sent me some of his sandals to be repaired last week. You never know when the centurion might have need for replacement sandals," Longinus said with a smile of his own. "We can't have the commander running around here barefooted, can we?"

Mario shook his head. This young man definitely had potential.

Longinus washed his hands and arms, smoothed back his hair, adjusted his tunic, and was ready to go with Mario in a matter of minutes. The rest of the leather-shop crew grinned and gave him the "thumbs up" sign.

That evening, Julius and the others had eagerly gathered around him. As Longinus recounted the day's events, his excitement had been contagious.

"The centurion accepted the new sandal design and the nail pattern too," Longinus said. "In fact, he directed that *all* new and replacement sandals for the entire century be made this way. He wants us all to have this hobnail pattern as a distinctive mark of who we are. When we transfer out of the unit, the sandals will be reminders of this century," he said triumphantly.

Good-natured laughter and backslapping had rippled through the tent as the soldiers celebrated the command. After all, they had had a part in the idea and ownership in the outcome.

"How soon can we have the new sandals?" surged a chorus of voices.

"We want them first," chimed in Julius.

"OK, OK," responded Longinus with a grin. "Our eight-man unit will be the first—*the very first*—of all the troops in the century to have the new sandals. I'll start to work on them tomorrow. Of course, the centurion gets his second pair before any of us get ours. We have to take care of him," Longinus laughed.

"Fair enough," responded the rest of troops. "We'll help you cut the leather and will even help you work on the nail pattern, if you'll teach us how. We can do it before the evening meal and after the sword training. That's free time for us, and no one will be upset. After all, we are a team."

"We'll leave our mark on the world!" Longinus told his friends with a smile. *Yes,* he had reflected, *being in the legions and making sandals and making friends is far better than staying home in a little village with my father.* Here, he had found camaraderie, acceptance, and teamwork. He had found meaning for his life.

As Longinus and Julius drew near the end of their march that day and near the end of their leave, Longinus's thoughts returned to the present. He looked down at his feet. He was still wearing those sandals, and they were leaving their marks on all the roads he traveled. And, he realized, even as the sandals were leaving an impression on the ground, the military was leaving an impression on his heart and mind. His life had changed. *He* had changed.

Questions for Thought and Discussion

1. When has your life, work, or experience taken a positive turn in a direction that you didn't expect? What was that like for you? What are the outcomes for you?

2. The *optio* saw leadership potential in Longinus. What marks of leadership do you look for in people as you assess their potential?

3. It often takes courage for leaders to step up to the plate with new ideas. Recall a time when you did that. What were the results? Where do you see positive potential to lead right now? How and when will you step up to the plate?

4. Most organizations have some type of chain of command. Do you see that as functional or dysfunctional? Explain. Where are you in this chain? How attentive are you to those you oversee or supervise?

5. What creative contributions and ideas are brewing in your mind right now that might make a difference in your home, workplace, or church? How and when will you help those come to fruition? Outline a step-by-step process for that.

6. The Romans left impressions on their world with coins, roads, buildings, sandals, and other things. What kinds of impressions are you leaving for—or on—others? How are you doing that?

Chapter 7

THE COLLISION

The leave Longinus and Julius went on had been great. The wound on Longinus's arm had healed completely, and his arm was nearly as strong as it had been. Longinus knew that with a few weeks of drilling and working in the leather shop, it would be as strong as ever. So, yes, Longinus had enjoyed the leave. But now he was glad to be back with his unit again. He loved the discipline, the camaraderie, the challenges, and the order that he had found when he became a Roman soldier. He appreciated too the recognition and rewards that came with the hard work of being a military man. Oh, to be sure, there were difficult days and grueling assignments. But he was growing—building up his body, his soldierly skills, his leadership abilities, and ultimately, his *career*.

Yes, his *career*. He had to smile at himself at the thought. At one time, he would have been incredulous at even the suggestion that he might have a career in the military. Back in his days as a trainee, his focus was on just surviving the rigorously long days and the training that Aquinas had piled on.

He could hear the rough voice of Aquinas even now. One never forgot his basic training or the tough-as-nails soldier who provided it. His face, his voice, and his name would remain with his trainees forever. The rough times, the tough training, and the pushing that Aquinas had done had made Longinus what he was today. And for that, Longinus was grateful. The impressions left by his first military trainer were both instantaneous and permanent.

Longinus could still hear Aquinas saying, *"Follow your heart."* And now, strangely, Longinus heard his heart saying "career soldier." He decided that this was what he wanted to do for the rest of his life. He was doing what Aquinas had said. He was following his heart. He was also following his head. He knew that Rome treated retired soldiers well, so making a career of the military could be a wise decision.

In his reverie, Longinus hadn't focused on where he was walking. Passing the corner of the supply building, he collided with a young woman. Amid the thud of falling scrolls, he heard her shriek, "What are you doing, you idiot? Watch where you're going!"

She bent to retrieve the scattered documents from the gravel path. Longinus noticed that her manner and clothing showed that she was no scullery maid. She was well-dressed, her red-auburn hair tied with beautiful ribbons.

Longinus sputtered an apology as he reached to help her pick up the scrolls scattered at his feet. "Here, let me help you pick up your things—it's the least I can do," he said, his face burning red with embarrassment.

"The less you help me, the better it will be!" she scolded. "You've done far too much already! Just leave me alone. I can do it myself. I don't need your help."

Her words were as pointed and sharp as a javelin, making Longinus blink in shock. As he reached to put the scrolls he had retrieved into her basket, she turned and fixed him with a green-eyed glare. Longinus froze, his jaw dropped to the "I'm catching flies" position, and his heart nearly stopped when he saw her face. He gasped in shock and recognition. He wanted to say or do something intelligent, but his mind and tongue just wouldn't work. The best he could do was stammer, "I . . . I'm . . . I'm so sorry. I didn't mean . . . I didn't think I . . . you were . . . I was . . . I mean . . ."

He could feel his face burning, as if he'd had spent a week in the bright sun. He felt, sounded, and looked like an embarrassed schoolboy.

The woman's fierce gaze melted into a wry smile as she cocked her head and looked at him. "Oh! I remember you!" she said with a coy smile. "You gave me back a scroll that I dropped riding my horse near Saalburg several months ago. Do you always use scrolls to meet people?"

Longinus just stood there, scrolls in hand, open-mouthed. She was as stunningly beautiful as he had remembered from their first accidental encounter.

Remember? Oh, yes, he remembered her! A thousand times his thoughts had wandered to their chance encounter, to her bright-green eyes, to her red-auburn hair, to her voice. Remember? How could he ever forget her? And now, here she was again—only inches away.

"Yes, I remember you," he finally managed to say. "I'm so sorry. I was thinking of something else and not looking where I was going, and I—"

Smiling, she reached out and touched his arm gently. "No apology needed. I could have been paying more attention too."

Her gentle touch jolted Longinus like a bolt of lightning. No, it wasn't a destructive, scorching thing, but a strangely warming, energizing sensation he had never experienced before. He stammered, "At least let me help you pick up the scrolls," and he dropped to his knees and began to gather more of the scrolls that lay scattered across the path.

"Thank you," she answered softly. "You can even help me carry them to my destination, if you wish. I would appreciate it—it would be nice to have an escort through all these military men." Her voice was as gentle as the breeze; her soft laughter like a mountain stream bubbling over moss-covered stones.

Longinus was awestruck. He gladly helped her pick up the remaining scrolls and put them in the basket. He asked, "What are you doing in this camp? It doesn't make sense for a young woman like you to be here with all these soldiers. Women aren't supposed to be here unless they work here. You certainly don't look like you work here."

The woman's smile widened, and her eyes began to sparkle as she responded, "Oh, I live in the camp. I've probably been around the military longer than you have. By the way, is your name Longinus? It seems to me I remember that from our last encounter. Is that correct?"

"Ah . . . yes . . . that's my name. I'm surprised that you remember."

Longinus noticed that when she spoke, she had an air of confident dignity mixed with genuine friendliness. He was even more amazed at the inner beauty that shone through her pleasant looks and personality. He wondered just what she meant, when she said she had "been around the military longer" than he had. She was truly an amazing person, and he was captivated by her.

"Well, don't just stand there! You offered to carry the scrolls for me, so here they are. Let's go," she said, as she thrust the basket into his hands and started to walk off.

The Collision

Hmm, Longinus thought to himself, *she has no problem taking charge in a situation. Where is she going?* He realized he had better walk faster and do less reflection if he were to keep up with her. He lengthened his pace to close the distance between them. Confident, she was. His curiosity grew with every step. And although he felt a bit foolish following her like a puppy, he was glad he had run into her again. She was an enigma—strong and bold, yet personable and funny all at the same time.

Obviously, she knew her way around the maze of streets in the camp. It was also obvious that many of the soldiers in the camp recognized her. The way crowded knots of men parted as she approached them told Longinus that he was right. She was no scullery worker or camp follower. She had some kind of standing to get the deference the soldiers showed her. There were no smart or vulgar remarks, no smutty smirks.

The longer they wound their way through the camp, the more his curiosity was aroused. She greeted various people along the path, and they responded to her readily. Several times he was about to ask her more about herself, but just as he got up courage to do so, she would say something to someone along the way and he had to build his courage all over again. So, he decided that for now he would just be silent and observant. He had the feeling that if he tried to push her in any way, the results wouldn't be positive. For now, just being with her was quite enough.

Longinus was so focused on her that he barely noticed where they were walking. When she stopped, he realized that they were at the entrance to the area reserved for high-ranking officers of the legion. He had never been to this part of the fort before. He had been summoned to the commander's office but never had any reason to go deeply into "officer country," as it was known by the troops. This was the place where the decision makers and their families lived.

Suddenly, he felt as obvious as a cat in a kennel filled with hounds. His clothing marked him as a line soldier, not a high-ranking officer. He was sure that everyone around was wondering, *What is that fellow doing* here? It seemed to him that judgmental eyes followed every step he took. He had started the trek thinking he was protecting this young woman. Now, he wasn't so sure but that the roles had been reversed. She was obviously comfortable and known here. He was the intruder.

The Centurion

Like all armies before it, the Roman system had rigid lines of rank and command. The commanders commanded, the regular soldiers carried out the commands, and the two groups didn't mix, mingle, or associate. High-ranking civilians assisted the commanders in a wide variety of assignments. They were free to associate with the commanders—a group known as the *equites*.

Originally, the *equites* were nobles. They came exclusively from the upper class, depending on their wealth and prestige to maintain the family name and position in the community. During the time of the Punic Wars, these nobles were accorded equestrian status. The term originated with the reality that to be a nobleman, or a knight, the individual had to have enough wealth and land to own his own horse. In later Roman history, the military supplied horses to those who were nobles, but the name *equestrian*—and hence, the elite status—followed them as a special designator of their standing within the Roman community and military.

Longinus quickly realized that the young woman he was walking with must be a daughter of one of the equestrian-rank men in the camp. Just as he realized this, she turned, smiled at him, and extended her hands for the basket of scrolls Longinus was carrying. "Thank you, Longinus, for helping," she said sweetly.

"The pleasure has been mine," he responded with a smile. "However, it seems unfair that you know my name, and I don't know yours." Longinus was a bit startled at his own boldness, but he'd made the comment and couldn't recall it.

"You're quite right," she responded. "Our meeting in the past was so fleeting that I failed to share my name with you. I'm Julia, the daughter of Gaius Metellus. Perhaps you've heard of him?"

Heard of him? Of course, Longinus had heard of him! He was a well-known businessman in the camp—a wealthy nobleman at the service of the camp commander. Gaius Metellus was the man who managed not only the nearby salt mines but *all* the salt mines in the territory protected and monitored by the legion.

The Roman senate had early discovered the value of salt—a commodity sought after by everyone in the empire, Roman and non-Roman alike and thus universally valuable. It was often used to pay for services in the place of silver or gold coins. Because of its value as a preservative, a flavoring, and a medium of exchange, Rome made a point to capture, hold, and control all the salt mines in the empire.

Refined salt was stored in a special area called the *salary*. Occasionally, it was said that someone was not "worth his salt." The comment was clearly understood to mean that the individual had not earned his pay—that he was worthless.

Now, things began to fall in place for Longinus. It became clear why Julia behaved the way she did, dressed the way she did, and presented herself with such dignity and confidence. It also made sense that she was an expert rider and had a beautiful horse. Her ability to read the scrolls and the quality of the literature they contained also spoke of her social status and upbringing. *So,* Longinus thought to himself, *I was right when I concluded that she wasn't one of the ordinary workers in the camp. She's far more than ordinary in every way.*

Julia smiled, reached out her hands again, and repeated her request for the basket of scrolls. Longinus handed them to her, returned her smile, and said, "It's been a pleasure to accompany you to your home. I hope that we can meet again sometime." Immediately after he said it, he regretted his boldness with such a beautiful woman who held such a high social standing.

Julia accepted the basket of scrolls from Longinus and turned to go. Longinus thought, *That's it, you dummy. She'll leave you standing here like a stupid pigeon. You've been too bold, and now you'll never see her again.*

But much to his surprise and delight, Julia turned to him with a smile and said, "I would like that very much, Longinus. Where do you work in the camp? I'll send one of my servants to fetch you, and we can take a lunch to a beautiful spot I know not far from the fort. We can both ride my horse—you aren't afraid of horses, are you?"

While Longinus had never really ridden a horse before, he wasn't afraid of horses. In fact, he admired them greatly. He had long dreamed of owning one himself. Anyway, he'd be willing to ride a lion in order to have lunch with Julia, if that's what she wanted.

As calmly and casually as he could, Longinus responded that he would be delighted to have lunch with her. He would, however, need to know in advance so he could arrange to be away from the leather shop where he worked. If she would let him know the plans, he would see to it that he had free time.

Yes, indeed, I will find time, make time, or pay for someone to fill in for me—whatever it takes. I will do whatever is necessary to have time with this lovely creature, he thought in delight.

Julia smiled sweetly and said, "I'll send someone with a message the day before we plan to have lunch together. Don't worry about the food. I'll take care of that. I believe you'll like my cooking." And with that, she turned and was gone.

Aha. Food. Longinus hadn't even considered food. He and his tent mates sometimes ate at the general kitchen but mostly cooked their own provisions in their barracks area. But what they cooked and how they cooked it was, well, "bachelor food." Many meals were barely edible, and Longinus wouldn't know what to fix for a picnic lunch with a lady. He was grateful for her offer to supply the food.

Longinus just stood there for a moment, awestruck at the encounter and the potential for future encounters with Julia. He very much wanted to talk with her more. The sound of a voice he recognized behind him broke his reverie. "Can I help you find your way, soldier? It looks as if you are lost."

Longinus turned to see Quintus, his centurion and commander, standing a few feet from him.

"No, sir, I'm fine, sir. I was just helping a young lady to her home. I'm leaving for my barracks right away, sir."

Quintus smiled and said, "I saw you with Julia. She's a cultured, refined young woman. You are fortunate to have made her acquaintance. It seems as if she rather likes your company too."

Longinus was dumbstruck. He absolutely didn't know what to say.

Quintus stepped forward, put his hand on Longinus's shoulder, and said, "Don't worry, lad. I'll vouch for you with her father. Gaius and I are very good friends. We've known each other for years. His wife died several years ago, and Julia has taken it upon herself to assist her father in his salt business and in his domestic affairs. She is a very capable young woman, and I consider her to be like my own daughter. Your reputation is sterling, and I shall convey that to her father. I expect you to keep her honor, your honor, and my honor clearly in mind in this relationship. Do you understand?"

Did he understand? *Of course,* he understood. It couldn't have been made clearer had it been written across the sky in flames. He also gratefully understood that the gods had smiled on him. He understood that his commander was willing to be much more than a commander for him in this situation. He understood the deep respect Quintus had for Gaius and his family. Longinus also clearly understood that he was to treat Julia with absolute and total respect—not that he would ever think of treating her any other way. His commander had said he thought of Julia as his own daughter. OK. That was a warning that even a stick of wood could understand. Now, many things began to come into perspective.

"Yes, sir, I do understand. I will respect her and her family as I respect you, my commander. Thank you, sir, for your understanding and advice."

"I wasn't trying to be nosy, but I couldn't help but overhear her invitation to you to have lunch with her. I'll speak to the leather-shop supervisor and inform him that while you will be expected to do your full quota of work, you will be given free time as needed to do 'special projects' for me. Your supervisor will understand that you have my permission to vary your hours of work as long as you accomplish the tasks that are assigned to you," Quintus said with a raised eyebrow. "How does that sound to you?"

"Thank you, sir. My work and commitment will not diminish," said Longinus.

"I'm sure that's the case, Longinus. Your cooperation, creativity, and hard work have been observed by those who directly supervise you, by my *optio,* and by me. All of this has earned our respect for you. Don't let us and yourself down."

Longinus had a feeling that his centurion was speaking to him more as a father to his son than as a commander to a soldier. Oh, to be sure, Quintus was still very much a commander—no question existed about that. But the tone of his voice and the look in his eye were deeper than that of a superior merely giving orders to a subordinate. His concern for Longinus was evident—as was his concern for Julia and her father. Longinus began to see a very human side of his commander, and what he saw only increased his loyalty and commitment to him. In this new situation, Quintus seemed to be the father Longinus had always wanted but never had.

And did he ever have a tale to tell the seven other soldiers in his barracks when he returned! They wouldn't believe it, he was sure. He could hardly believe it himself!

"Julia. Julia." He kept repeating her name to himself. It was like music to him. He didn't quite understand all the emotions racing around in his head, but that was fine. He would enjoy them anyway. And somewhere he seemed to hear the faint but clear voice of Aquinas saying, *"Go with your heart."*

Well, maybe this could be part of that mantra. Time would tell.

Questions for Thought and Discussion

1. Name some of the people in your past who have helped shape you. How did they do that? What words, actions, or behaviors made them memorable to you?

2. What prompted your decision to do what you have chosen as your lifework? Was it a quick choice, a slow process, or a combination? What place does divine guidance play in your decision to do what you do?

3. Recall an "accidental" encounter that had a lasting effect on your life. How did it change you?

4. Longinus realized that Julia was from a different class than he was. What are some class distinctions and divisions in your culture or location? Do those class boundaries serve a positive or negative function? How can you help someone feel more comfortable when he or she may feel like a commoner in "officer country"?

5. Quintus, Longinus's commander, could have nailed Longinus for being in an area he wasn't supposed to enter. Instead, he cut Longinus some slack. Has something like that ever happened to you? How did it make you feel or respond? Who "cut you slack"? Who needs you to "cut them some slack"? How and when will you do that?

6. Can someone be both a superior and a friend at the same time? Elaborate on your response.

Chapter 8

LIFE CHANGES

Nearly two weeks had passed since Longinus had literally run into Julia and stumbled into the hope that he might be able to develop a friendship with her. He hadn't heard from her since, and he was reviewing every word they had spoken to each other to see where things might have gone awry. He assumed that they must have gone awry since she hadn't contacted him, and he wasn't about to wander into the area where she lived without an invitation.

No word, no message, no picnic, and no idea what to do—it plagued him. At first, he'd thought the gods had smiled on him by putting the two of them on a collision course. Now, he felt that the gods were laughing at him for being such a fool as to believe she would be interested in him.

Longinus struggled with what he should do. *If I try and contact her, she may think I'm pushy. That would offend her,* he thought. *On the other hand, if I don't contact her, she may think I have no interest. That would be worse.*

Aquinas's advice echoed in his thoughts: *"Listen to your heart."* Well, he was trying to listen to both his head and his heart. The problem was the conflicting advice he got. He seemed to have run into a rigid, stone-walled dilemma.

The manager of the leather shop had been reassigned shortly after Longinus had run into Julia. Quintus saw to it that Longinus was appointed to take over that position. The promotion raised his pay and status, but that hardly mattered to him. Julia mattered to him.

The Centurion

In his spare time, Longinus had begun crafting a set of soft, supple leather saddlebags to give Julia. He knew her love for horses, and he wanted to share something he had created with her. The saddlebags would be a masterpiece of leatherwork and very valuable. But what if . . . ?

One evening, after the rest of the workers had gone back to their barracks, Longinus was nearing completion of the project. The final touches would be brightly polished silver decorations on the closure flap of the bags. As he labored to get the placement just right, he felt a tap on his shoulder. He hadn't heard anyone come in, so he was startled and whirled around, nearly scaring the messenger boy to death. The lad jumped back, wide-eyed, as though he had touched a hot coal rather than Longinus's shoulder.

"I . . . I'm looking for soldier Longinus," the boy stammered. "I was told I could find him here."

"You startled me, but that's all right," responded Longinus, wanting to calm the boy. "I am Longinus. What can I do for you? Do you need something repaired?"

"No, sir. I have a message for you from Lady Julia," said the lad, and he thrust a small scroll toward Longinus.

Longinus's pulse quickened, and he reached for the scroll. As soon as he took it, the messenger bolted out the door and down the path.

Longinus noticed that the scroll had been sealed with the finely engraved ring Julia wore. He hesitated. What if the note said, "Leave me alone, you low-life"? What if . . .

What if he just opened the message? Then he would know what it said. He carefully pulled the ribbon from the wax seal and unrolled the scroll. In fine, precise writing it said:

> Congratulations on your promotion to manager of the leather shop. Please join me tomorrow just before midday for lunch to celebrate that promotion. I will send my messenger to guide you to the glade where we shall eat.
>
> My apologies for the delay in contacting you. I have been away on business with my father. I hope to see you tomorrow. Julia.

Could he meet her? Was the sky blue? Was rain wet? Of course, he could meet her! He quickly finished the saddlebags, wrapped them in a cloth, and fairly floated back to the barracks.

The next day, Longinus could hardly wait for the appointed time. He had assigned the other workers to do the work that needed to be done, and they had smiled and agreed to do what he asked of them. While they didn't yet know why Longinus was so happy, they liked him and were willing to follow his directions. He treated them fairly, and they were glad to have him as their foreman. Their cooperation confirmed the truth of that age-old saying, "If the boss is happy, we are all happy."

The lunch was delightful, the day was wonderful, and feasting his eyes on Julia was delicious. She was witty, smart, beautiful, composed, and, best of all, she was there with him.

As they enjoyed their meal, they talked about their likes and dislikes, hopes and joys. Julia told about her mother's death and her taking up of the role of helper to her father in his management of the salt mines.

"Do you remember that scroll you found and returned to me near Saalburg?" she asked.

"Of course, I remember," responded Longinus. "You seemed glad to get it back."

"Yes, I was!" she said. "It was the record of all the salt rations and distribution for the next month, and I was frantic to find it. It would have taken me an entire week to reconstruct it. You saved me hours of torture. I never thanked you adequately, I fear. I was so relieved to get it back that I just rode off and left you standing there."

Oh, yes, Longinus remembered very well.

"So," she continued, "this lunch is a part of my saying thanks to you."

Longinus was quick to pick up on the words, "*part* of my saying thanks." He wondered what that might include.

Julia smiled at Longinus and said, "Let's make this lunch meeting a regular thing every week. Would you like that?"

Would he like that? Oh, by all the gods of the pantheon, he would love it!

"Yes, I would very much like that," he responded and then added, "I haven't been around women much, but I think I'd like to learn that skill. I'd especially like to learn it from you."

After the words were out of his mouth, he regretted them, thinking he might have been too bold. He blushed and looked away.

Julia noticed his red face. "You look good in a suntan," she said, laughing. Somehow that put him at ease.

"Here," he said, drawing out the cloth-wrapped saddlebags he had made. "I know how much you like to ride horses. Maybe this will keep you from dropping any scrolls for someone else to pick up."

Julia's eyes went wide with delight as she unwrapped the package.

"I made them myself for you," Longinus said. "They're from the best leather available and are soft so they won't damage the scrolls. I hope you like them."

"I do like them!" she exclaimed, adding, "and I like you, too."

The lunch time was over far too quickly, but Julia had to get back to helping her father, and Longinus had to get back to the leather shop. In the months that followed, their lunches together became the highlight of Longinus's week—and were also the talk of the leather-shop workers.

Quintus informed Longinus that he had talked with Gaius, and the salt manager trusted Quintus's observations about trooper Longinus and his intentions toward Julia. "She's strong-minded," Gaius told Quintus, "so I am glad she has taken interest in a man who has leadership potential in the legions and who is a decent person. I'll let her decide where the relationship goes."

Quintus told this to Longinus, and he was amazed at Gaius's open-mindedness. Many Roman fathers, like Longinus's own father, ruled their families with an iron fist, insisting on deciding whom their children would associate with and especially whom they would marry. Apparently, Gaius was not that kind of man. And Longinus took Gaius's attitude as a major clue as to how he should relate to Julia. She wanted to be with someone who treated her as an equal, not someone who ordered her around like a servant. She expected respect and mutuality, not patronizing or domination.

As their friendship continued over the next several months, Julia and Longinus both realized that they wanted to be much more than friends. Julia was attracted to Longinus's moral strength, industriousness, and integrity; and he was attracted to her clear thinking, strong-mindedness, and inner as well as outer beauty. They were under no illusion about the rigors of being married while Longinus remained in the legions. But Julia was comfortable with those challenges, having been raised in the shadow of military camps. Longinus had found his niche in the military. His identity, focus, future, and fortune called him to a career in the Roman army.

Julia discussed her feelings at length with her father, and he quite agreed with her about Longinus and the potential of their future together. As the resident manager of the salt mines in various locations, he had dealt with a large number of people. He was a shrewd man and had learned to read others well. Frankly, he liked what he saw in Longinus—a man who wanted to serve Rome and the emperor. Longinus was someone who was moving up the ranks because of his ability and effort, not because he wanted to show off.

Eventually, in a burst of bravery, Longinus arranged to talk with Gaius about his desire to marry Julia. Longinus had come to appreciate Gaius, but he still felt the distance between himself and Gaius and his standing in the community.

When Longinus said he wanted to marry Julia, Gaius smiled and replied, "Longinus, you are young both in age and in your military career. I know that. Julia knows that. And Quintus knows that. However, we all agree that you have the potential to have a great future. I couldn't find a better husband for Julia than you can be. You have my blessing and my approval.

"But . . . ," Gaius said, and at that word Longinus felt his heart leap into his throat. "But," Gaius repeated, "Julia has the last word in the matter. You have my permission to ask her to marry you, but the final decision will be hers, not mine, and she knows that is the case."

Longinus was thrilled at Gaius's acceptance of him. He had a plan for how and when he would ask Julia to be his wife. In most of their luncheon outings, she had prepared and brought the food. This time, he would reverse it and invite her to a lunch he would be responsible for. He arranged to have the best cook in the camp prepare the food, bring it to a place he had chosen, and set up a feast for just the two of them. Then Longinus would bring Julia to this special place and, after they had enjoyed the meal, ask her to marry him. Longinus asked Julius to make the final arrangements, and he assured Longinus that there would be no unpleasant surprises.

So, Longinus invited Julia to join him for a special feast marking their sixth month of friendship. He informed her that he had made all the arrangements and that she should meet him at the camp gate just before noon the following Sunday.

The Centurion

When they arrived at the location for the feast, she was surprised at the beautiful setting and arrangements. Longinus had selected a spot on a grassy place near a clear stream. A cloth had been spread on the ground for them to recline on as they ate, and delicious food awaited them in covered baskets. Julius had come through, as Longinus knew he would.

They enjoyed the meal, talking freely about what had happened through the past week. When they had eaten their fill of the various desserts they found among the baskets, Longinus cleared his throat, took one of Julia's hands in his, looked her in the eyes, and said, "Julia, I want our friendship to last forever. I ask you to be my wife, if you are willing to marry a soldier."

There was an eternity of silence as Julia looked down and began to pluck blades of grass from the turf. Longinus waited for her response with eager anticipation and absolute vulnerability. If she said No, he was sure he would die on the spot. If she said Yes, he was afraid he would explode with joy.

"Well, Longinus," Julia said, drawing out her response in what seemed to be calculated deliberateness, "the thought has crossed my mind too, and . . ."

Julia paused, and Longinus's heart raced.

"And what have been your thoughts, Julia?"

"I have questioned the wisdom of being married at all. And I have looked at the hard life of an army wife, moving from fort to fort and place to place. Raising children in that environment would be a challenge . . ."

Longinus felt his mouth go as dry as though he had it packed with sand. Maybe he should have waited to ask, maybe he—

"I've thought a lot about it," she continued with a frown. Then her gaze jumped from the blades of grass to Longinus's eyes as she said with a smile, "and my only thought is that being married to you would be wonderful. Yes, I will marry you! In fact, I was planning to ask you if you hadn't gotten around to asking me soon."

With that, Longinus let out a whoop of glee, jumped to his feet, lifted Julia up, and embraced her tightly.

"Julia! You had me sweating for a moment there. You are a tease as well as a marvelous woman!"

"And you are a marvelous man," she whispered in his ear. "I'm eager to have you as my husband."

Then Longinus fumbled in his cloak and brought out a small item wrapped in linen. Julia watched as he carefully unwrapped a delicate, beautifully engraved bronze ring that he had brought as a symbol of their engagement.

"Julia, I promise myself to you in marriage. This ring is a symbol of that pledge for all to see and for you to know my intent," he said as he slipped the ring onto the third finger of her left hand. The ring's placement reflected Roman belief that a nerve ran from that finger directly to the heart. Longinus meant his pledge with all of his heart.

There was great celebration in Gaius's home that evening as Julia told her friends about her pending marriage to Longinus. And on the other side of the camp, in Longinus's *contubernium,* Longinus's band of brothers celebrated too. "We'll be glad to get rid of you," they teased.

The wedding was set for June—the time of year the omens said was best for such events. The wedding would be held in the house of the bride's father. Roman norms dictated this location for the wedding ceremony, which portrayed a transfer of control of the bride from her father to the groom—not that Gaius, Julia, or Longinus saw it that way. But Gaius's villa was beautiful, so that was a major factor in favor of the traditional location.

Julia would be dressed in a white gown with a veil, and her attendants would also be veiled. The veils were used to confuse any evil spirits that might be lurking about and trying to harm the bride. Julia's dress would have an elaborate belt around her waist tied with the knot of Hercules, which was considered to be the guardian of wedded bliss. The knot was to be untied only by the groom; he would untie it after the completion of the marriage festivities.

The ceremony consisted of the two standing in the presence of the camp priest and holding hands while repeating the traditional marriage chant: *"Quando tu Gaius, ego Gaia,"* meaning, "When and where you are Gaius, I then and there am Gaia." This chant was deeply rooted in the historical meaning of the name *Gaius,* which was considered to be a lucky name. All brides and grooms said this chant no matter what their names were.

Ten witnesses would be there to hear the couple exchange their vows and to assist the bride and groom as they then offered cakes on the altar of Jupiter. After the chant was spoken and the offering made, the guests ate the wedding feast at the home of the father of the bride, marking full recognition of the union.

The Centurion

The feast was one of the key elements celebrating the marriage. Longinus's *contubernium* group, his commander, Quintus, and several others selected by Gaius from among his friends served as witnesses for his and Julia's marriage.

Following the wedding feast, Longinus led Julia to their new home, just outside the fortress walls, where she again repeated the chant as he picked her up and carried her over the threshold into their new home while guests threw nuts to symbolize their wishes the couple have a fruitful, child-filled marriage. Marriage was a civic duty for Roman citizens, as was the bearing of offspring to keep the empire populated.

Julia used the torch that had lighted the procession to their new home to start the first fire of their married life on the hearth. Once that was done, she extinguished the torch and tossed it to the waiting guests to bring them good luck too.

The fort commander had given Longinus two weeks off to celebrate his marriage, so the newlywed couple had ample time to enjoy their new status before Longinus had to resume his work in the leather *fabrica*. When their honeymoon was over, Julia returned to her work as assistant to her father, while Longinus continued directing all things having to do with leatherwork in the fort. He still had to participate in all the military training just as the other soldiers did, but he could live outside the fort when not engaged in military matters.

Some six months after the wedding, Julia approached Longinus one evening after their meal and told him she had an announcement.

"And what would that be?" he asked.

"Try and guess," Julia responded with a sweet smile, baiting him.

"You want to redecorate the house?"

"That's part of it. What else?"

Longinus was never good at these kinds of exercises, but she was obviously fishing for him to come up with something. He tried again.

"Your father doubled your wages?"

"No, silly!" she laughed, her voice like a melody. "You're going to be a father. I'm pregnant."

Longinus just sat there, not knowing what to say. They had talked about having children, but it had seemed so remote, so far in the future. Now the future had arrived, and he simply didn't have the words to respond.

"You are happy about this, aren't you?" Julia asked with some concern in her voice.

"Of course!" Longinus replied instantly. "I just thought it would take longer. I mean, do we have enough room? . . . There are so many things to prepare. . . . I don't know how to deal with children. Of course, I'm delighted . . . and afraid too!"

"As far as needing more time," she said, "it will be seven more months. I guess that's all the time we will have."

"I can work with that," Longinus said, grinning from ear to ear. "I'm going to be a father!" he kept repeating to himself, his joy growing and his fear abating.

The pips on this ring may symbolize the wearer's wish for divine guidance and protection where he was and at all points of the compass.

The intervening months passed as fast as a spring rainstorm. When the baby was born, one more critically important Roman custom came into play. After the midwife had delivered the baby, she gently took him from Julia, wrapped him in a soft cloth, and took him outside, where Longinus waited with a group of witnesses. The midwife then laid the child down on the ground, unwrapped him, and stepped back with anticipation.

Longinus now had a critical decision to make. He could either reject the child by turning away from him, or pick up the child, leaving the cloth on the ground.

If he turned away from the child, he was denying any responsibility for it, and the child would lie there until some other person picked it up and took it home or until the child died of exposure. In nearly all cases, rejection by the father meant death for the child.

If, on the other hand, the father picked the child up and held it, he would proclaim to all the witnesses that he accepted both the child and the responsibility of providing and caring for it.

Longinus gladly and quickly picked up his son. In his joy, he willingly accepted his son and all the responsibility that came with him. The midwife and witnesses clapped and shouted their approval.

Longinus's next act was to proclaim the name of the boy he held in his arms. He and Julia had already decided to name him Gaius Julius, in honor of her father and Longinus's best friend. Their joy seemed absolutely complete.

Julia knew, however, that at any time, Longinus could receive orders sending him to some remote corner of the empire. Concerned about his safety, she gave him a bronze ring that she'd had made by one of the best bronze workers in the area. The design on the square flat face of the ring resembled the number five face of a die. There were dots within circles in each of the four corners of the face and a dot-circle in the middle. The dots and circles represented the eyes of the gods. The ring was Julia's prayer for the gods to be with her soldier-husband north, south, east, west, and wherever he would go.

Questions for Thought and Discussion

1. Longinus waited for two weeks to hear from Julia. How hard is it for you to wait for an answer about something that's important to you? What kinds of things go through your mind while you wait? Describe what it was like for you to wait for an answer from God. What was the occasion? What was the outcome? How does this relate to the second coming of Christ?

2. What has been a pleasant surprise for you recently? Share the details and circumstances. Who could you surprise in a positive way this week? How and when will you do that?

3. Who should make the decisions in a relationship, partnership, or business? What process should be followed? How is leadership defined and decided in these settings?

4. What are some specific gender roles and stereotypical rules in your family, workplace, church, or community? How do they help or hinder progress there?

5. What qualities attract you to other people? What qualities of yours do you think attract others to you? Why?

6. Recount your engagement and wedding. How similar were they to the Roman customs in this chapter? Relate what you see of Roman wedding customs in Matthew 26:27–29 and Revelation 3:20, 21; 21:1–5. What new insights does this give you?

Chapter 9

GAIUS BECOMES AN ADULT

The years passed rapidly. Longinus rose in rank to *optio* and then to centurion. By that time, Pilate had moved into the circle of the emperor and had married the emperor's daughter, Claudia Procula. The emperor assigned Pilate to Judea, and, in turn, Pilate called both Longinus and Julius into his service as partial fulfillment of the promises he had made after they saved his life. During those years, Julia's father had died and she had inherited his fortune. So, Longinus and Julia were more than comfortable—they lived well.

Shortly after Julius and his wife, Livia, moved from Capernaum to their new posting in Jerusalem, Julia went there to visit them. While she was there, Julius invited Livia and her to come to the stable to see a foal he had acquired recently. The wobbly legged, skinny colt was hardly a beauty. But Julia could see beyond the presently unimpressive animal to what it would become in the future.

"Do you have plans for that colt?" she inquired.

"Yes, indeed I do. I have big plans for this colt. This ugly animal will develop into one of the best of all my holdings," Julius replied, smiling.

"Hmm," mused Julia. After a reflective moment, she said, "Longinus and I have been thinking that we might purchase a colt soon and have him trained so that when Gaius turns eighteen, we can give it to him. Are you sure you can't sell that colt to us?"

Julius laughed. "You certainly know a good horse when you see one, Julia, there's no doubt about that. But as I said, I have plans for this colt—very special plans."

"Such as?"

"You don't give up easily, do you?" teased Julius.

"Not when it comes to a fine horse or a fine family," answered Julia with a grin. "So, what 'special plans' do you have for this gangly colt?"

"Do you really want to know?" Julius asked with a mischievous grin.

"Of course. Why else would I press you so?"

At this, Julius began to chuckle.

"What's so funny?" asked Julia. "You know I won't give up without an answer from you."

"Longinus was right," Julius returned, with a smile.

"Right about what?" Julia queried with an upturned eyebrow.

"Oh, about your good taste in husbands—and in horses."

"Horses are more predictable than husbands," responded Julia, smiling sweetly. "But let's not get off the subject of this colt's future."

"Here's the plan," confided Julius. "Six months ago, Longinus asked me to keep my eyes open for the best colt in Jerusalem—the *very best colt in the entire city,* not just any mount. I was to let him know when I had found the animal. When I spotted this colt, I knew I had found what Longinus was looking for."

"Longinus asked you? I don't understand."

"He had the same thing in mind that you do—a special horse for a special young man. Of course, Longinus told me that you would have the final say. He trusts your judgment totally. And if you want this colt trained for Gaius's eighteenth birthday, it will be done. That's part of the understanding we have."

Julia's eyes sparkled with delight as she said, "So you two super centurions have conspired—"

"Not actually conspired, but we did plan for a special birthday gift—this very horse. So what do you think?"

"This colt will be just right! He's exactly what I—we—have in mind. So how much silver will it take to buy this colt, and who will train him?"

"Both the price and training are covered," said Julius. "It's our gift—mine and Livia's—to you, to Longinus, and specifically to Gaius."

"But this colt is valuable!"

"True. But good friends are more valuable than stacks of silver. I've already spoken to Pulcher about training the colt for Gaius. He'll train it for the next two years. Pulcher is the best horse trainer in all legions."

"Yes, but this colt is worth far too much for you and Livia to give it away," Julia protested.

"Livia and I want to give this horse to Gaius. You and Longinus are our best friends, and Gaius is like our own son. He even carries my name. We wouldn't have it any other way."

A warm smile spread across Julia's face. Her eyes danced and sparkled with excitement, as she gave Julius a big hug. "I, we, accept your offer gladly. There's no way we can thank you enough for your kindness," she fairly sang.

"Our joy will be full when we see Gaius ride that stallion when he reaches adulthood," Julius said. He smiled as Livia nodded her head in agreement and then gave Julia a big hug.

"Julia," Livia added, "your friendship means more to me than you'll ever know, and we feel that helping you with this surprise for your son is like our giving this horse to our own son."

"What about a trainer, though?" Julia asked. "Is Pulcher well enough to train the horse? It hasn't been long since he was close to death. If it hadn't been for that healer, he wouldn't have pulled through."

"Pulcher is fine," Julius answered. "As good as new—maybe better than ever. He's ready to start training the colt as soon as it is mature enough to be trained. And if we have the training done here, Gaius will have no suspicions about the horse, and the surprise can be complete."

The two years passed quickly, and soon the long-awaited day arrived. Gaius was turning eighteen. On his birthday, he would take off the cloak that minors wore and don the toga of an adult Roman citizen. The day would mark his transition from childhood to adult life, adult freedom, and adult choices.

Julia smiled as she recalled the conversation she'd had with Julius and Livia two years before. Everyone had kept the secret. Gaius had no idea he was about to become the owner of a beautiful stallion, although he had often mentioned that he wanted to have his own mount.

Julia had taught Gaius to ride when he was only ten. Then, he was a skinny, awkward child. He'd been as gangly as the colt was two years ago. Now, however,

Gaius Becomes an Adult

Gaius was a strikingly good-looking young man. He had his father's muscular build and dark hair and Julia's intense eyes and attention to detail.

Julia had been an exacting trainer. Her father had taught her to ride when she was ten, and she was determined that her son would be an excellent rider as well. And her training had not been in vain: Gaius had been an apt pupil, and he was an excellent rider. In fact, he was a better rider than most of the soldiers who guarded Pilate when he left his villa to attend to state business. Julia was deeply proud of him.

As a special honor, Pontius Pilate and Claudia Procula were present for the birthday celebration. They had been told about the stallion, so they had arranged to have a saddle custom-made as their gift to Gaius. The saddle was made of supple black leather that had been imported. It had been tooled by the finest leatherworkers in Caesarea and had unique bronze rosettes trimmed with silver. The black leather of the saddle and its bronze and silver appointments looked stunning against the sleekly groomed coat of the stallion.

At the appointed time, servants pulled back the curtain across the entrance to the banquet room as Longinus, in full and finely polished armor, stepped into the room. He raised his right hand for silence. "Your honor Pontius Pilate, honored Claudia Procula, and distinguished guests," he said. "I am pleased to introduce to you, Gaius, the newest adult in Caesarea. May he live long and serve our emperor well."

As Gaius stepped through the doorway, the guests applauded and chanted, "Live long and serve Caesar well! Live long and serve Caesar well!"

Gaius smiled as he accepted the accolades of the guests. Julia beamed, observing that he looked stunning in his adult tunic. Longinus agreed with her. They were extremely proud of their handsome and accomplished son. Longinus recalled the unhappiness he had experienced with his own father and their ugly parting, and he was delighted that he and his son had a strong, positive relationship. Not only were they father and son, but they were solid friends as well.

The birthday celebration was to include a sumptuous meal, but before the servants began to bring out the food, Longinus stood up and clapped his hands to gain the guests' attention. "Ladies and gentlemen," he said, "before we dine, I want you to join me on the balcony for just a moment."

When the guests moved to the balcony, they saw a regal stallion bearing a stunning saddle tethered to the hitching post below. As Gaius joined his parents and the guests on the balcony, Longinus could hardly contain himself. He looked at him and said, "That horse, my son, is *yours*! He's been thoroughly trained and is ready for you to ride and care for. Welcome to adulthood!"

The guests applauded their approval as Gaius went slack-jawed with surprise. "Really?" he exclaimed. "It can't be!"

"Oh, yes," said Julia, "it is true. The horse is a gift your father and I planned for you—but it's really from Julius and Livia. And the saddle is a gift from Pontius Pilate and Claudia Procula."

Gaius's face was as radiant as the rising sun on a cloudless day as the reality dawned on him that this was indeed his horse. At first, he seemed rooted to the spot where he stood. That changed quickly. In a flash, he was down the stairs and beside the horse, stroking its sleek side, speaking in soft tones to it, and examining the splendid tack and saddle. The horse gave a slight whinny of approval and nuzzled his new master. They seemed to bond immediately.

"Now, friends," Longinus said, "let's return to the tables to enjoy the rest of the evening. I doubt that Gaius will be joining us for a while. I'm sure he wants to become better acquainted with his horse."

Yes, it was a special day—a very special day. Nothing could have made it better. Everything had gone exactly as Longinus and Julia had planned. They were pleased, Gaius was delighted, and the guests were enjoying the party. Even Pilate seemed at ease. It seemed that on this day Longinus, Julia, and Gaius were beginning a new era.

Questions for Thought and Discussion

1. What were some of the transition markers you experienced in moving from childhood to adulthood? How did those affect your life? Were surprise gifts part of that celebration? How did that make you feel?

2. Longinus and Julia, along with their friends Julius and Livia, sponsored a dinner to mark Gaius's transition to adult standing in the community. What can you plan for young about-to-be-adults in your family as they reach their "majority"? (Remember that "family" includes your work associates, church, and community friends.)

3. What would or could be some indicators of or celebrations for reaching spiritual maturity?

4. Where are you in your spiritual maturity right now—preschool, grade school, adolescent, young adult, or adult? Explain.

5. What is your plan for reaching the next stage in your spiritual maturity? How will you celebrate the transition?

6. How can you support and celebrate the growth toward spiritual maturity of those closest to you? Who are they?

Chapter 10

THE ACCIDENT

"Longinus! Come quickly," shouted Porius as he ran toward Longinus, who was sitting at his desk.

"What is it?" asked Longinus, looking up from the maps of Jerusalem he was studying in preparation for a visit there by Pilate.

"It's your son, sir. There's been an accident at the stable. Come quickly! Please sir, come quickly!"

"What happened?" Longinus asked as he ran with Porius to the stable.

"Several of us were in the stable with Master Gaius. We were preparing for a group ride and *spatha* sword drill in the field. Master Gaius asked if he could join us, and of course, we said he could. He saddled his horse and joined us. Just as we were leaving the compound, the horses bolted. There was a snake by the gate. Master Gaius's mount reared up, and the master fell to the ground. Then the horses just went wild with fear and began kicking, and sir, it was terrible!"

"What? What was terrible?"

"Sir," continued Porius, "before Master Gaius could get out of the way, his horse kicked him in the head. He's badly injured. We tried to help him, sir, but it all happened so fast, we couldn't do anything about it. I'm so sorry, sir."

As Longinus and Porius approached the stable, they saw a group of soldiers kneeling around Gaius. Lucius, the unit physician, was already there, gently cradling Gaius's head and wiping blood from his battered face.

When the physician saw Longinus approaching, his eyes spoke more loudly than his hushed voice. "It looks bad, very bad. You'd better call his mother. We'll take him to the infirmary immediately. We'll do all we can, but . . ." His voice trailed off into silence.

Porius volunteered, "Sir, I can send someone for Mistress Julia. You best stay with Gaius."

"No, but thank you for the offer. I need to tell her myself," Longinus responded grimly as he turned toward his quarters. After taking a few measured steps, Longinus broke into a trot and then into a full run.

When Julia spotted him running toward the house, she knew immediately that something was very, very wrong. Longinus's face showed it. He'd never been one to mask his feelings. He was always who he was—up front and honest.

Julia asked, "What is it?" The words were sharp with anxiety.

"I—I don't know how bad it is, but Gaius has been hurt in a riding accident. They're taking him to the infirmary right now. Dr. Lucius and Rufus are with him. We must hurry to the infirmary."

"How did it happen? When? How badly is he hurt?" Julia's questions revealed her concern. Deep furrows of concern marred her face. Longinus explained the situation as best he could while they rushed to the infirmary together.

By now, word of the accident had spread through the camp like a wildfire through a stubble field. The soldiers made a wide path for the couple as they hurried to the infirmary.

The guard at the door quickly snapped a fist to his heart in a salute as Longinus and Julia approached. When Longinus returned the salute, the guard spoke. "I pray the strength of the gods to be with you, sir." Startled, Longinus blinked and stammered a thank you as he and Julia rushed into the infirmary.

When Julia saw Gaius, she gasped and her hand flew to her mouth. Gaius lay limp and still on a blanket-draped cot. Both eyes were swollen shut. Bright-red blood oozed from his mouth and nose. And you could see the partial outline of a hoof print on his forehead and crushed cheek.

"Doctor," croaked Julia, barely able to speak. "Is he alive?"

"Yes, but he's badly injured. You can leave him here or we can carry him to your quarters. There's nothing more we can do."

Tears spilled down Julia's face as she touched her son's curly brown hair.

The Centurion

The doctor had washed most of the blood out of his hair, but when she withdrew her hand, it was covered with fresh blood. Obviously, the injury was indeed very serious.

Julia turned her tear-streaked face toward Longinus, her eyes pleading for him to make it right. The commander of troops longed to do so, but this was a situation well beyond his control. He gently took her hand and turned toward the doctor. "Take him to our home," he directed. "We'll go with you."

The physician and attending soldiers gently lifted Gaius onto a stretcher and carried him to the family quarters.

"What can we do for him, doctor?" Julia asked.

"Keep him warm and put cool cloths on his face and head to reduce the swelling. That's about all anyone can do," he responded.

He paused, weighing his next words carefully and then said as gently as he could, "I must tell you the truth: the wound is serious. It will take a miracle for him to recover. We'll do what we can, but there are limits to what a physician can do. I'm sorry."

Longinus was a good commander and a good man. No doubt about it, he could be a tough commander, but his soldiers cared about what he cared about because they knew he cared about them. Their loyalty to and concern for him was as deep as his loyalty to and concern for them.

And Gaius was a favorite of the camp. He was the age of many of the younger soldiers, and many of them identified with him. And to many of the young troops, Longinus was a father figure as well as being the commander of troops. So, the grief and concern of the soldiers was as real as the grief and concern of the parents.

Longinus's troops soon began to implore the gods for the healing of their commander's son. Those who followed Mithra began their elaborate rituals in hopes that the gods would intervene on behalf of Gaius. Others, Cybele's followers, slipped silently from the camp, and in the darkness of night sharpened their knives and then cut their own wrists as a blood offering for the well-being of their commander's son. Although their wounds were superficial, their intent was serious. They willingly gave of their blood for the restoration of the wounded young man.

For Longinus and Julia, the first of many long vigils began that night. They took turns watching over Gaius. He moaned a little but didn't speak or move.

Occasionally, during his watch, Longinus would gently squeeze cool water from a sponge into Gaius's mouth. As he did, he said over and over, "I'm here for you, Son, I'm here. I won't leave you."

During those vigils, Longinus often questioned their decision to give the stallion to Gaius. "Don't," Julia objected. "That's what Gaius wanted when he came of age. You and I both know he is an excellent rider. And the horse is well trained. No one is to blame. Don't blame yourself. It was an accident."

Longinus found comfort in Julia's wisdom and steadiness. He was always amazed at her strength as well as her beauty. Neither had changed since the first time he met her many years ago. In fact, both seemed to become richer every year.

Likewise, Julia drew strength from Longinus. He was a good man, a good leader, and a good husband. They both needed each other. They also desperately needed a power beyond themselves to help their son.

One night, Gaius's eyes flickered and opened. "I'm thirsty," he mumbled.

Longinus responded immediately, gently lifting his son's head and giving him some water.

"Father, forgive me," Gaius muttered. "I should have been able to control the horse."

"Shhh," replied Longinus, "don't blame yourself!"

"Father . . . Father . . . Don't leave me," Gaius pleaded. Then his eyes closed again, and he returned to that vast gray twilight between life and death.

Longinus reported Gaius's moment of consciousness to the doctor and to Julia. Both were encouraged that the boy had opened his eyes and spoken.

One day when they were alone together, Julia asked Longinus, "Do you remember what I told you that Julius did when Pulcher was so sick?"

"No, not exactly."

"It was when Julius and Livia were in Capernaum, just before Pilate put him in charge of the troops in Jerusalem," Julia said.

"I remember your mentioning something about Pulcher having been sick," replied Longinus. "What did Julius do?"

"He went to a rabbi—a young man named Jesus, and Jesus healed Pulcher."

"What are you saying, Julia?"

She hesitated only an instant and then replied, "I think we should see if

Julius knows how we can contact Jesus. Maybe—maybe this Jesus can help Gaius too."

"You can't be serious!" responded a wide-eyed Longinus. "Me, the commander of Pilate's troops, asking a Jew to do his hocus-pocus on our son? That would be unthinkable, Julia! We have one of the best doctors in the empire right here in this camp. Lucius is the personal physician for Pilate and Claudia Procula. He's doing all he can—all that any doctor could do—for Gaius.

"And why on earth would we even consider asking a rabbi for help? These Jews are nothing but trouble. That's why I am here—to help Pilate control them and keep the lid on this steaming stewpot of a place called Judea. If there is a cure for Gaius, it will come from a Roman doctor, not from some Jewish fraud."

"But," stammered Julia, "I saw a little of this Jesus the last time I visited Julius and Livia in Jerusalem while you were traveling with Pilate. Longinus, this man Jesus isn't a 'Jewish fraud,' he's—"

"He's what?" snapped Longinus.

"He's caring and compassionate and good, and—"

"Stop! Stop right now, Julia! Enough of this talk—the answer is No. I won't consider it. I won't discuss it."

"But they say he's performed miracles. Lucius said that it would take a miracle for our son to be healed, and—"

"Julia," Longinus's voice softened a bit, "have you abandoned your senses? Are you telling me that you have more faith in a miracle-working Jew than in the wisdom of Rome?"

Julia slowly hung her head. Tears ran down her face like small rivers, and her chin began to quiver.

"Look, I'm desperate too!" continued Longinus. "I love our son more than life itself, but we must trust our own physicians and not rumors about some obscure rabbi."

"What about Pulcher?" Julia asked somewhat defiantly, her eyes flashing with that fiery "I'm in charge" look that had attracted him to her. When she was upset, as she was now, her eyes could fairly spark with a determination not to be ignored or pushed away.

"All right, I'll give it more thought," Longinus responded. Julia knew that really meant the discussion was over. Longinus wouldn't consider inviting a non-Roman to see his son. His pride in the power of Rome was too strong to bend to any other culture or belief.

There was a knock at the ornately carved door of their house. It was Lucius. "I thought it would be good to check on Gaius," the physician said when Longinus ushered him in. "How is he?"

"The swelling has gone down some, but he's not responsive. That concerns me," Longinus said. "And he's had only water and a little broth."

As they entered the dimly lit room, Julia gently stroked Gaius's hair. Then she turned toward them and said, "His breathing scares me."

Lucius examined Gaius carefully. Then he slowly shook his head and said, "Things don't look any better."

"What more can we do?" whispered Julia.

"Only wait," replied Lucius. "To be honest, Madam Julia, it is up to the gods at this point."

Suddenly, Gaius's eyes opened, and he said in a raspy whisper, "Mother . . . Father . . . I . . ." Then his eyes rolled back, he took one deep breath, and lay completely still. The battle was over. The gods hadn't intervened.

Julia's face was contorted with anguish and pain. Longinus felt his body go cold with shock. He took Julia in his arms and held her as she sobbed.

Longinus felt like he had been punched in the stomach. Death was no stranger to him. In battle, he had delivered death to enemy soldiers. He had marched to the gates of death himself, looked through the bars, turned around, and come back. But this was his own son. The blow was crushing, nauseating, and overwhelming.

The next hours and days were a blur, each blending into the other. Julius and Livia came to Caesarea from Jerusalem to give support during the funeral ceremonies. Pilate and Claudia came to pay their condolences. Longinus's troops expressed their support. Even Pulcher came. With tear-stained cheeks he told them how much he had come to love Gaius. He assured Longinus that he had done everything possible to train the stallion for the young man and that it was one of the best-behaved horses he had ever handled.

Longinus was touched by his former tormentor. Pulcher seemed a very different man. He had changed. Oh, to be sure, he was the same big burly bunch of muscle he had been when he and Longinus had first sparred with each other back when they were trainees, but his demeanor had softened, his coarseness had been refined. Now Pulcher had a depth to him that surprised Longinus.

An honor guard from the legion, in full military armor, led the funeral procession to the burial plot. A temporary stone marker was already in place at the gravesite. It would later be replaced by a finely carved monument, as was fitting for the son of a centurion. The marble monument would note the life and death of Longinus's and Julia's son, but nothing could take away the crushing pain they felt.

Julia avoided the subject, but Longinus couldn't help wondering whether things might have been different if he had sent for that rabbi, the one who had healed Pulcher—whatever that rabbi's name was. *Don't be ridiculous,* he reasoned with himself. *We did all we could. Rome's best attended Gaius.* But still, the thought rolled through his mind: *What if . . . ? What if . . . ?*

Questions for Thought and Discussion

1. Recall a time when tragedy struck a family member or someone close to you. What kinds of reactions and responses did you see and experience? Which is more difficult to deal with: a lingering death or an abrupt and unexpected death? Explain.

2. Longinus's troops turned to the gods they knew for help. How have you turned to God for help in tough or tragic times? How can you touch others with spiritual help and support in their need?

3. Reflect on the aspect of human nature that seems to compel us to find someone to blame when there is a tragic accident. Discuss John 10:10 in light of your thinking and reflection.

4. What do you need to say to a friend or family member right now before they die, concerning how you feel about them? What is your plan to follow through?

5. Longinus was fairly abrupt with Julia when she asked about sending for the Rabbi who healed Pulcher. Why do we sometimes turn others away when there is a tragedy?

6. If the family had sent for Jesus, do you think He would have responded? Why or why not? When you face tragedy or stress, will you call for Him? Why or why not?

Chapter 11

SEARCHING

After Gaius's death, Longinus threw himself into his command responsibilities even harder than before. However, while he wasn't at all lax with his soldiers, some saw him as having become a bit mellower. Yet he was still in every way the commander of his troops. Work was the way he dealt with his loss. Keeping busy kept his mind off Gaius and the pain burning in his soul—a pain that touched everything in his life.

Julia was still heartsick too. She was managing her loss well. But some days, the redness of her eyes betrayed the smile and warm greeting she gave Longinus when he came home after being with the troops on long training marches. Longinus and Julia often talked about their life together and about their son. They spoke of the joy he had brought into their home and of how much they missed him. What they didn't say was how deeply they still hurt. As the weeks and months passed, the immediate pain lessened some, but the loss was still raw and real.

One day, Julia told Longinus that she was thinking of visiting Julius and Livia in Jerusalem. "They have done some redecorating, and I'd like to get some ideas and perhaps even find some of the materials they used," she said.

"That sounds like a good idea," Longinus responded. "In fact, there is a big Jewish festival coming up in several weeks—I believe it's called Passover. Pilate plans to go to Jerusalem with Claudia Procula during the time of that festival. That means I'll going there too. Why don't you go ahead of me? You can spend time with Julius and Livia, and then, after the festival, we can all return to Caesarea together."

"All right," said Julia with a sparkle in her eyes. Then she added, "Maybe after your Passover detail, you can take some time off, and we can visit the seacoast near Tyre and Sidon or go somewhere else just to get away. You haven't taken any time off in quite a while, and we could use a break—a second honeymoon, a new beginning."

"It's true that I've been pushing pretty hard lately. I'll ask Pilate about it. A change sounds welcome to me as well, and I like the idea of a second honeymoon," Longinus said with a smile.

Both Longinus and Julia realized their need to get away. Although it had been nearly a year since their son's death, at times the salt-in-the-wound memories were still raw and painful. Some time together away from the familiar surroundings would be welcomed by both of them.

They had noticed that sometimes memories returned without any warning. Just the week before, Longinus had been headed down a dusty path by the troop barracks, intent on making sure that the troops were preparing provisions, armor, and wagons for the Jerusalem trip. Suddenly, he had stopped dead in his tracks and let out an audible gasp. He'd caught a glimpse of one of the new recruits and for an instant thought it was Gaius. The way the young recruit threw his head back and laughed with the others, the way he moved, the way he held his shoulders—all reminded him of his son. The impression had taken his breath away. He heard his heart pounding hard against his ribs and felt the quickened heartbeat throb in his head. Then the pain of loss hit him again like the barbarian's battle club.

Longinus hadn't told Julia about what had happened. He feared it would only upset her. But his father's heart still longed for his son and still greaved at the loss he had experienced. He wondered if things like this happened to Julia too, or was it just to him?

Yes, he reflected, *it would be good—and helpful—to create some new, positive memories.* Julia's idea of a seaside trip was appealing. He would enjoy relaxing by the Mediterranean Sea, with its warm, sandy beaches and beautiful palm trees. He wasn't going to let his emotions get out of hand. He was, after all, the commander of troops, so he determined that he would be in charge of his feelings as well as of his soldiers.

Longinus tried to stay focused on his work and not his feelings. But in spite of his determination, his thoughts turned to Gaius at times. Then he began to bring to mind the various religious practices he'd explored as a young military man. He knew the most about Mithraism. He had gone through the levels of *corax* ("raven"), *nymphus* ("bride"), *miles* ("soldier"), and *leo* ("lion"), and had reached that of *perses* ("Persian") when he lost interest in the cult.

As Longinus reflected on his journey into Mithraism, he began to recall some of its teachings. The cult taught that Mithra, the sun god, was the Orphic creator god who emerged from the cosmic egg at the beginning of time and then brought everything else into existence.

It was the cult's portrayal of Mithra as the action god of armies and the champion of heroes that had attracted Longinus when he had enlisted in the Roman army. The "champion of heroes" aspect of its teachings had strong appeal for many other soldiers as well.

Another of the cult's central teachings was that Mithra had died, been buried in a rock tomb, and then had resurrected to life again. Since the loss of his son, the idea that Mithra was a resurrected and *life-giving* god had a powerful pull for Longinus. The loss had created a vacuum, an emptiness, a hole in his being that he desperately wanted to fill. He thought that maybe he should look into renewing his quest to move up the ranks of Mithraism through the next stage, *heliodromus* ("sun-courier"), and on to the most respected and highest rank within the cult—the most exalted level in Mithraism, the level of *pater* ("father").

The soldiers at Caesarea had built several *mithraeum*—centers of Mithra cult worship. Most of these centers were small natural caves that had been adapted by adding raised benches along each wall that seated thirty or forty soldiers. A recess at the end of the cave held an altar on which incense was burned, and lamps gave a flickering, ethereal light to the worship center.

Caves were used because of the myth of Mithra's death and burial in a rock tomb. They were also said to represent the cosmos. The caves were adorned with images of the sun, moon, and various constellations: a serpent (Hydra), a scorpion (Scorpio), a dog (Canis Minor), and Corvus, the raven—all signs of the zodiac. The place of honor was given to a representation of Mithra killing a sacred bull—which was the constellation Taurus. All of these symbols offered the hope of eternal life to the worshipers. Of course, the promise of resurrection and eternal life was especially appealing to those who regularly faced death in combat. So, Mithraism's popularity with the troops grew in proportion to their exposure to combat.

The worship of Mithra, the god of armies and champion of heroes, was limited exclusively to men. Worship consisted of a ritual meal at the meetings. There were no holy scrolls. A high-ranking member, usually the *pater*, introduced the lower-ranking members to the rituals they needed to learn to advance to the next level. They, in turn, mentored those below them. The small size of each "congregation" built a tight-knit camaraderie that added to the *esprit de corps* of the military units.

Mithraism originated in Persia, but that didn't trouble the Roman soldiers who became devotees. Even the emperor supported Mithraism, because it supported the concept of the emperor's divinity. Mithra was the giver of authority and victory to the house of Caesar. Maybe, Longinus thought, he would even be the source of authority and victory to him. But even more interesting to Longinus right now was the hope of understanding—and experiencing—death and resurrection. *Yes,* he thought, *after Julia and I get back from Jerusalem and have a few weeks off, I'll take another look at the worship of Mithra. It can't hurt, and it may give me the answers I need. There may be a whole series of new beginnings for us—answers to the questions that trouble us, and peace for the pain we're experiencing.*

So, Longinus decided he would put this quest aside until after the trip to Jerusalem with Pilate for the Passover. Work must come first. It always came first. Then things would be different. He just needed to get beyond this next assignment in Jerusalem. Then everything would change.

Questions for Thought and Discussion

1. While reactions to loss and grief vary greatly, some have said women tend to deal with pain by talking about it, while men tend to deal with those issues by throwing themselves into their work. Do you agree or disagree? Cite examples from your experience or observations.
2. Longinus bottled up his feelings inside himself and didn't discuss them with Julia. Is that a good idea? Explain.

3. When have you seen or experienced the "just get away from here and it will all be OK" way of dealing with loss? Does it help or hinder?

4. Flashbacks such as Longinus experienced are fairly normal in trauma situations. They can become dangerous when the person experiencing them can't distinguish "then" from "now." When have you seen or heard of this kind of imbalance due to flashbacks? How can you assist someone who is experiencing pain from the past due to flashbacks?

5. How have you dealt with—or how are you currently dealing with—losses and pain in your life? Who can help you with that? How can you help someone experiencing grief or loss?

6. List some biblical texts and stories dealing with grief and loss.

Chapter 12

TO JERUSALEM

Three weeks had passed since Julia had left for Jerusalem to visit with Julius and Livia. *Just as well,* thought Longinus. *I need to put in some very long days with the troops in order to be ready for the Jerusalem trip with Pilate. We wouldn't have much time together, anyway.*

Pilate called Longinus in early one morning to check on the readiness of the troops and the preparations for the trip to Jerusalem.

"Sir, the troops are ready. They have been trained, toughened, and prepared for any threat to you, Claudia, or the emperor," responded Longinus with a sharp salute.

Pilate smiled and expressed his appreciation to Longinus. A unique bond existed between the two men. It had been seeded when Longinus and Julius had saved Pilate, who had been their commander, from death on the battlefield. But there was more to it than that. Both Pilate and Longinus were committed career professionals in the service of the emperor. Both were proud to be working to-gether.

Their individual paths had taken different directions after the incident with the barbarians. Pilate had gone on to serve Emperor Tiberius directly, and there he had met and married Claudia Procula, the emperor's daughter. After their wedding, the emperor had dispatched Pilate to Judea, where he became the procurator of that historically unruly province. As such, he was the personal representative of Rome and of the emperor in all of Judea.

The path Longinus had taken led him through service all across the Roman Empire. Eventually, Pilate had made true on his promise to both Longinus and Julius, by arranging important assignments for both of them. Longinus had become commander of Pilate's guard—a small, personal army. And Julius had been assigned to Capernaum. But when Pilate came to Caesarea, he called Julius to Jerusalem to be the commander of troops *SPQR*—"for the senate and the people of Rome."

Because the meeting with Pilate was a formal briefing, Pilate wore his formal white toga over his standard white tunic. The toga was a real work of art. Pilate's was made of the finest imported linen. It was eight feet long at the bottom edge, which was straight. The opposite edge was an arching curve that, at the apex of the arch, measured eight feet from the bottom. Black-and-gold laurel-leaf trim ran all along the bottom border, the laurel leaves being symbols of victory. The toga was intended to be impressive, and it was. It informed everyone that the wearer was wealthy, powerful, and extremely important.

Pilate also wore the golden laurel-leaf crown that Tiberius Caesar, his father-in-law, had given him. Although he didn't need to wear it for the briefing with Longinus, it was customary to do so. Pilate was, after all, the official representative of Rome, and he wanted to look every inch the part.

Longinus had prepared for the meeting, too. His armorer had rubbed down his armor with sand to remove any blemishes and then polished it with a fine film of oil. The bronze hinges and fittings had been buffed to a golden sheen, and the copper rivets shone like spots of red flame. Longinus's helmet had also been burnished to a mirrorlike sheen, and the crest had been replaced with a new one. The curved base of the crest followed the line of the helmet exactly. It was made of wood covered with a thin sheet of bronze. A luxurious brush of white horse-tail trim extended nearly six inches above the crest box. A flowing, blood-red cape trimmed in black and gold completed the centurion's formal dress.

The helmet and crest made Longinus seem even taller than he actually was, thus adding to the "I am the commander" impression. Together, Pontius Pilate and his commander of troops, Longinus, made a strikingly powerful visual image of strength, control, and presence for Rome and the emperor. The crest also served in helping the troops identify the centurion to whom they should listen for orders. This was especially true in combat, when there would be competing orders and general confusion. The crest made it easier to find your commander and not be sidetracked by someone else.

Pilate had another order for Longinus. "One more thing, my friend. You are to take the robes of the high priest from my quarters and personally deliver them to Caiaphas when we get to Jerusalem. The high priest cannot officiate at the Jewish rituals without those robes."

"Yes, sir, I understand. I will secure the robes and will deliver them as directed."

"Actually," responded Pilate, "Order him come to you. Let's emphasize the fact that Rome is in charge. Let's remind him that he functions as high priest only because we allow it. He may be the high priest, but we're in control."

"I understand fully, sir," responded Longinus with a smile. "It will be my personal pleasure to let him know that Rome still rules."

"Is it true that Jerusalem is the only major city in the realm that doesn't have a statue honoring the greatness of Emperor Tiberius?" Longinus inquired.

"Yes, it's true, and it's an insult to the emperor. I sent troops into Jerusalem a few years ago carrying standards with the likeness of Tiberius. It caused a riot. It had something to do with the Jews' beliefs about 'graven images' or something along that line. They called it 'idolatry' and raised such a ruckus that we had to kill many of the rioters to quell the uproar. Caiaphas and his father-in-law, Annas, were stirring up the crowd. I have no use for either of them, nor do they for me, I suspect. No matter. Rome is in charge, and we'll remind Caiaphas of that," Pilate said with a scowl.

As Longinus left Pilate's quarters with the high priest's robes, he couldn't help but reflect that Tiberius's only son Drusus had died and Tiberius had been forced to adopt Germanicus and to groom him to be the next emperor. But Germanicus had died too and that left Tiberius with no blood relatives to succeed him to the throne. So Emperor Tiberius might formally adopt his son-in-law, Pontius Pilate. That would put Pilate in line to be the next emperor. Roman law was clear: Roman fathers could disown their natural-born sons who displeased them, as Longinus's father had done to him many years before. But once adopted, a Roman son was secure forever. His father could never disown him. Never. Adoption was absolute and permanent.

If Tiberius did adopt Pilate, and if Pilate became emperor—well, the very thought brought a smile to Longinus's face. He could potentially become the military commander of the entire Roman army! He and Pilate already had a positive professional relationship. They understood each other. They trusted each other. Longinus had clearly and often proved his loyalty to the emperor and to Pilate. Longinus smiled again at the very real possibility of becoming the commander of the entire Roman army—a pleasant thought indeed.

It actually did look as if Tiberius was contemplating the adoption of Pilate. Just recently, he had dispatched Marcellus Sylvanus, one of the sixteen official augurs in the Roman Empire, to observe in Pilate's court.

Pilate thought so highly of dream interpretation and augury that he had augury symbols included on all the coins he had minted. Two of his small bronze coins, the *lepta,* had the symbol of the augur's staff on them. The *littus,* or staff of the augur, was a long piece of wood with a curve at that top resembling the gentle curve of the chambered nautilus shell. The form of the staff represented the unfolding wisdom and knowledge of omen interpretation said to reside personally with an augur.

The *littus* identified the bearer as a Roman augur, or omen interpreter. The mathematically perfect curve symbolized the perfection of omens and revelations from the gods.

Augurs served as the interpreters of omens at the royal courts and in the Roman senate. The ruling elite would begin no major undertaking—personal or political—without first consulting with an augur. No major decision would ever be made without first consulting the signs—*auspices,* as they were called— for an interpretation of omens from the gods. It was believed that the emperor ruled Rome by the will of the gods. The gods revealed their will to the emperor, and the emperor ruled accordingly.

Every Roman military camp had a special place known as the *templum* where the augur would observe the signs. The boundaries of this sacred location were outlined in the earth. Then the augur used his *littus* to mark an area within the *templum* that served as a sort of window encompassing earth, sky, and sea (if they were near the sea). Any omen that occurred within that space within a specific time period was considered to be communication that revealed the will of the gods.

When something, such as a bird, moved from right to left within the "window," that constituted a positive omen. Things that moved from left to right were considered to be negative omens. Other sky omens included cloud movements and especially lightning. Among the most powerful omens were the flight or landing of either an eagle or a vulture. All natural phenomena, such as earthquakes, meteors, thunder, and especially an eclipse of the sun or moon, were considered to be powerful messages from the gods. Dreams and visions were also seen as interventions of the gods—messages or warnings to those who ruled. Augurs interpreted the meanings of the omens.

Judea was widely considered to be the most trouble-ridden province in the entire Roman Empire, and consequently, the toughest to govern. If Pilate did well there, who could say he wasn't fit to be emperor—and thus fully fit to follow his father-in-law Tiberius as the next emperor of Rome? So, Longinus was sure that Pilate was paying attention to the augur he kept at his court. He looked to him to provide the guidance from the gods that would boost his success in governing Judea.

Right now, the omens were good. So, this trip to Jerusalem might well help to solidify both Pilate's governorship and his future. And this trip could solidify Longinus's future as well. Time would tell. One thing was sure: Longinus and his troops were ready for anything Jerusalem had to offer. Anything at all. And come what may, Longinus was completely loyal to Pilate and to the emperor. Nothing could or would ever change that.

Questions for Thought and Discussion

1. How does clothing show social or other rank? Is the saying "clothes make the man" true today? Why? How might it relate to the robe of Christ's righteousness that a Christian wears? How is your robe?
2. Roman commanders wore a crest on their helmet to make clear in the heat of battle to whom their soldiers should listen. How do we distin-

guish the voice of Christ from other voices in our daily battles?

3. Roman adoption was forever. How secure are you in being an adopted child of Christ? What gives you a sense of security about your salvation? How can you increase your sense of security and that of others around you?

4. What makes a person "system savvy" the way Longinus was? Is that a positive or a negative thing? Explain. What's the difference between being system savvy and being a smart aleck? How can you increase your system sense in the social and work realms and in the spiritual realm?

5. Romans believed the gods spoke through omens. How does God speak to people today? How does He speak to you today?

6. The Romans considered an eagle or vulture in flight to be one of the major omens. What might Jesus' statement in Matthew 24:26–28 have meant to a first-century Roman? What does it mean to you in light of what you know?

Chapter 13

THE AUGUR

Marcellus Sylvanus, the augur, kept pretty much to himself. His main job was to interpret for Pilate and his wife any omens and auspices that could affect their future well-being and that of Rome.

Marcellus had been conspicuously absent for about three weeks. Pilate would say only that he was "on a mission" of some sort. When Marcellus returned, Longinus found out that he had gone to Jerusalem to learn more about a rabbi who Pilate worried might be stirring up trouble for Rome. In light of the pending trip to Jerusalem, Pilate wanted Marcellus to look things over. He had apparently considered the mission important enough to keep it secret even from Longinus.

Longinus knew that Marcellus had frequently traveled incognito, dressing as an ordinary merchant, to check on potential troublemakers in and around Judea. Marcellus spoke Greek, Aramaic, and Hebrew, as well as Latin, so he could pick up information from all kinds of people in Judea—especially from those who had no idea he could understand their conversations.

Pilate invited Longinus to join him and Claudia when Marcellus gave his report. The meeting would be held in their richly decorated private quarters, where colorful imported silk banners hung from the white marble walls, giving a festive yet regal feel to the room.

"The rabbi I was investigating," Marcellus said, "has a strong following among the common people—fishermen and the like. But he has powerful enemies among the priests, Pharisees, and Sadducees. He is no threat to Rome. In fact, I believe he is quite mad."

"Tell us more," directed Pilate as he reached for an ornately decorated goblet filled with wine.

"I heard him say to the Pharisees and other leaders of the Jews that he would be some kind of a sign—an omen. He said that one day they would see him in the clouds in the sky. Imagine that—a man suspended in the clouds! That's sheer madness!" exclaimed Marcellus as he waved his hands in the air like billowing storm clouds.

"Strange indeed," observed Pilate. "What else?"

"Well, he also said that he would be 'lifted up' and that he would 'draw people to him,' whatever that means," Marcellus continued with a frown. "It makes no sense to me."

"He *is* mad," responded Claudia. "He must think he's some kind of magnet!"

At that, Pilate and Marcellus laughed heartily, Pilate nearly choking on his wine.

"There is more. He said that he would die and come back to life again, and then, when he came back in the sky, his return would be like lightning from east to west. He even said that he would also raise from the dead those who believed in him," replied Marcellus with a snort of disdain.

"You mentioned that he had enemies," said Pilate, as he poured a goblet of ruby-colored wine for Claudia.

"Oh, yes indeed. The leaders at the temple feel threatened by him, because he draws more attention than they do. It's a case of green-eyed jealousy. They certainly won't support him. They would kill him if they could, but he is far too popular."

"Your opinion of the situation?" Pilate asked.

"Sir, in my opinion, this rabbi is just another wild-eyed lunatic who does Rome a favor by drawing popularity and power away from the temple leaders. He's no threat to anyone—and certainly not to you, Excellency. He is a threat only to himself."

"Still, we probably should keep an eye on him. What is his name?" asked Claudia.

"*Yeshua,* in Hebrew. It's a common name. They call him Jesus of Nazareth.

He's from Bethlehem and Judea, originally. Now he seems to operate in and out of Capernaum."

Longinus didn't say anything. It wasn't his place to do so. He focused on picking up the details and remembering what was being said. But the mention of Capernaum, where Julius was stationed, caught his attention. He was curious. Could this be the rabbi who had healed Pulcher—the one Julia had wanted Longinus to send for after Gaius's accident? *It's a good thing I resisted that idea,* Longinus thought to himself. *Wouldn't it have been an embarrassment if I had invited a madman to my home! Pilate would have lost all respect for me.*

While Marcellus spoke of this teacher with utter disdain, Longinus was curious about him. His claim that one day he would be lifted up and that he would be in the clouds—that was the same as claiming to be endowed with supernatural power and perhaps to be divine. Even Caesar was careful not to make that kind of claim. Who was this Jesus anyway?

Longinus recalled the teachings of Mithraism that he had learned. An eagle in the sky was one of the most powerful of all avian omens. That's why the eagle was a symbol of imperial Rome. Longinus even had an eagle on his helmet to honor Rome and to seek the protection of the gods in warfare. Seeing an eagle in the sky was a jaw-dropping, eye-popping event for a Roman. A man in the sky? Impossible! Marcellus was right, this rabbi was no threat to anyone except himself. *He* is *mad,* Longinus thought with a smile.

Madness. You need not look for madness, reflected Longinus. *It will find you.* Just recently, one of his up-and-coming young centurions had become deeply involved with the cult of Cybelle. In his eagerness to find favor with the gods, the young soldier had paid for an expensive ceremony that was supposed to give him the strength and prowess of a bull and to make him as invincible as the gods. He had spent nearly three months' wages to purchase a sacred bull. He then paid to have a pit dug, over which a heavy iron lattice was placed. Next, the thrashing bull was dragged over the lattice and tied to it. Then the young soldier had taken his *pugio*—the standard military dagger—and slit the throat of the bull. Then he had crawled into the pit and bathed in the blood of the bull. What could be crazier than that? How could anyone believe that bathing in blood would improve *anything*?

Oh, to be sure, many religions taught and many people believed that life was in the blood. And it certainly was true that when someone was seriously injured in battle, one must stop the loss of blood or life itself would ebb away. But Longinus thought that to believe that life itself—the gift of the gods—could be transferred through blood was sheer madness. It was as bizarre as someone claiming that he would ride on a cloud!

But what did make sense? Gaius's death made no sense. He was such a promising young man—strong, smart, and sensitive. The best years of his life had still been ahead of him. He had just begun to live—to be a man, not a child. Then, he was dead, and the hopes and plans Longinus and Julia had for him were all dashed to pieces as a pottery vase shattered when smashed on a marble floor. It made no sense. It seemed that life was madness unfolding before you.

All the years of soldiering, the hard work, the training, the marching, enduring the rain and the wind, the cold nights in the field, the carnage of battle—sometimes none of it made sense. Even the promotion to the position of commander of troops for Pontius Pilate didn't bring the fulfillment Longinus had thought it would. So what *did* make sense?

Perhaps Marcellus knew. He would ask Marcellus. That made sense. Maybe Marcellus could bring some meaning, some order to Longinus's scrambled thoughts and emotions—especially regarding the death of Gaius. After all, Marcellus was one of the sixteen augurs in the Roman Empire. He was one of those rare and trusted official interpreters of omens. He wore the ring of the augur, with its engraved *littus* staffs, "eyes of the gods," and the lines representing the four basic elements of existence: earth, water, wind, and fire. These symbols proclaimed that the gods would reveal truth and give guidance through the augur—the spokesman for the gods.

Longinus shook his head and rubbed his eyes. *Snap out of it!* he told himself. *You have a job to do and troops to prepare for the trip to Jerusalem. There's no time for all this questioning of omens.* So, he determined that he would consult with the augur when this trip to Jerusalem was completed and after he and Julia had taken some time off. Perhaps Marcellus could help him find the answer to the nagging emptiness he felt.

As Longinus prepared to inspect the troops, he realized he'd better check his own armor. For all he knew, on this trip he might need the protection it offered, so it paid to make sure it was in good condition. And of course, he wanted to set the right example for the rest of the troops. What he did had major import.

The two *littui* shown crossed on this ring form two eyes of the gods, and the four dashes represent earth, water, wind, and fire.

Longinus had several suits of different types of armor to choose from. Typically, the commander of troops would wear a type of mail shirt with a double layer of links over the shoulders and an intricate system of leather straps worn over the mail. The straps held the commander's silver *phalerae*—the medals he had been awarded during his years of service. Or he could wear the muscled *cuirass,* a very ornate, two-piece set made like the Greek armor of the past. The front piece was formed like a heavily muscled male torso, while the back piece was plainer but somewhat muscular too. The two pieces were held together with leather straps, and a decorative ribbon wrapped around the waist to show the rank of the wearer.

Longinus preferred the banded armor he had worn as a young soldier. The other two kinds of armor had their place in parades and honor ceremonies, but he preferred the mobility of the banded armor. More than that, it was the type of armor his troops wore. By wearing the same type of armor, he was identifying with them. It was also a way of saying to them, "I've been where you are, and if you do well what you have been trained to do, you can be where I am."

As Longinus checked his armor, he pondered again the reports Marcellus had given Pontius Pilate about the young rabbi who was in Jerusalem. Was he the rabbi who had healed Pulcher? What about this "coming in the clouds," and being lifted up and drawing people to himself? And what about his claim—and this was the one that stood out most in Longinus's mind—the claim that he would die and then rise from the grave? Was that possible—to come back from the grave? Could Gaius live again?

Longinus shook his head and chided himself silently: *Enough of these wandering thoughts and ruminations on Marcellus's report. Why give a second thought to this mad rabbi who talks about riding clouds and lightning? It is total madness. Julia is right; I really do need a break! Our trip away after this Passover event will do me good. I hope it will clear my mind.* With that, he went back to his preparations. The trip to Jerusalem with Pilate was soon to take place, and there was work to do.

So, Longinus did as he had done many times before in his military career. He filled his mind with the work before him, crowding out his deeper thoughts and feelings. His job was what mattered—the *only* thing that mattered. His questions could wait until after the job was done. He was the commander of troops, and he would be in command of himself first of all. That way, he would be in command of any situation that might arise.

He was sure of that.

Questions for Thought and Discussion

1. Jesus' predictions of being seen "in the clouds" seemed like madness to Marcellus. What aspects of the return of Jesus seem like fables to people today? Why do you think people find it hard to believe some of the statements in the Bible about the Second Coming? How can you help them sift out the madness of inaccurate, nonbiblical ideas from accurate prophecy?

2. This chapter mentions the bloodbath *tarabolium* ritual as a way some sought to gain strength. What do you do to maintain your physical

health and vitality? What spiritual exercises do you do to maintain and increase your spiritual strength?

3. Longinus was supersuccessful by the standards of his culture, yet he felt an emptiness that he wanted to fill. Can you identify with that in any way? What have you seen others do—positively and negatively—to fill that void? How can you fill it?

4. The *littus,* the augur's staff, depicted an unfolding progression. What has been the unfolding progression in your spiritual life? Are you becoming more open or wound more tightly? What are you doing about it?

5. Longinus elected to wear the same armor his troops wore as a way of identifying with them. How do you form a link with those around you? Why do you do that? How does God identify with us today?

6. In the story, Pilate was deliberately playing power games and politics with the high priest. Have you ever seen those kinds of games going on where you work, worship, or live? What are the results? What have you learned from those situations?

Chapter 14

PASSOVER

Longinus suggested and Pilate agreed that the *optio,* Marcus, accompany Pilate and Claudia Procula on their trip to Jerusalem. Marcus would have the bulk of the troops with him. Longinus would go to Jerusalem a week early to make preparations for Pilate's entourage and to see for himself what the threat level would be during the festival. Longinus would also bring the high priest's garments to Jerusalem, as Pilate had ordered, so Caiaphas could officiate at the Jewish temple.

Caiaphas, the current high priest, was the son-in-law of Annas, who had been the high priest for more than twenty-five years before Pilate came to the area as procurator. Pilate's predecessor, Valerius Gratus, had appointed Caiaphas to his office. So, Pilate had inherited the high priest and could do little about it without stirring up a hornet's nest of problems—something he definitely did not want to do. The place was always in turmoil as it was; to deliberately stir up the people was not in his best interests. The control the Jewish high priest wielded was powerful indeed.

There were more than twenty thousand Jewish priests scattered from Jerusalem to Rome to Africa and India. Those priests had a powerful influence over all the Jews in the Roman Empire, and while the priests posed no overt military challenge to Rome, they could be a serious distraction if not an outright threat to the *Pax Romana.* At the pinnacle of this priestly pyramid stood Caiaphas, a man who hated the Romans with a burning passion—a man who loved pomp, power, pageantry, and the influence he held as much as any Roman emperor.

Longinus smiled to himself at the thought of his "unholy pagan hands" being in charge of the high priest's robes. When he reached Jerusalem, he sent a message to Caiaphas that he himself would need to come to the Antonia Tower to claim the robes; Longinus wouldn't release them to anyone else. In the message, he said that the high priest personally claiming the robes was a "matter of protocol."

In some ways, that was true. Longinus didn't want the robes to go missing, and that claim could be made if anyone other than the high priest came to get them. That charge could spark a riot. No, Caiaphas himself would have to come get the robes and even sign for them in the presence of witnesses as well. Longinus would allow no opportunity for problems to arise over the robes. He had them in his possession, and he alone would determine how, when, and under what circumstances they were conveyed to Caiaphas. If Caiaphas didn't like the terms, well, that was just too bad.

In preparing to fight a battle, a good commander must anticipate problems and make plans to eliminate them where possible. This "battle"—the power struggle between Caiaphas and Pilate—was to be waged with wits, not weapons. Longinus was as adept at this kind of battle as at the physical kind, and he was eager to show Caiaphas that a Roman commander was *always* in control, no matter what the setting or situation. It was a reality that Longinus wanted to reinforce on Pilate's behalf.

When Longinus's orderly told him that Caiaphas and his delegation had arrived to receive the robes, Longinus sent the orderly back to the delegation asking them to come into the guardroom of the Antonia Tower, which overlooked the temple complex. They could receive the robes there, and only there.

The orderly returned quickly to inform Longinus that the Jewish delegation declined to enter the Roman fortress due to their ceremonial rules. They asked that he bring the robes out to them instead.

This surprised Longinus. He had expected their refusal to enter the Roman building—it had something to do with the Jews' view of the Romans as pagans and thus somehow unclean; the priests might "defile" themselves by entering the building. This much Longinus knew, but how dare they demand that he come to them?

"No," Longinus said in reply. "If they want the robes, they come to me. Otherwise, I may use them to clean my horse—or at least, I'll have them returned to Pilate's palace in Caesarea."

Longinus's response was a threat, a challenge, and an order, all in one. He knew full well that Caiaphas must have the robes to officiate at the Passover events and that Caiaphas didn't want to enter the Roman fort. Longinus had deftly put the high priest into a well-calculated double bind. The thought caused a wry smile to break out on Longinus's face. He sat down and waited for a response.

"Sir, they agreed to enter and are waiting for you as directed," the orderly reported a few moments later.

"Fine. Let them wait," Longinus replied. "Tell them I'll be with them shortly."

Longinus was not about to miss an opportunity to make the point that he, a representative of Rome, was in charge. He would drive the point home as a hammer pounded a nail into a board, and then he would clinch it with one final blow in the power play. So, "shortly" turned out to be an hour. But, finally, Longinus picked up the robes, wrapped in the fine linen the high priest had himself wrapped them in when they were delivered to Pilate earlier in the year.

As Longinus entered the guardroom, the soldiers snapped to immediate attention. The high priest's entourage shuffled uncomfortably, their discomfort sharply increased by the movements of the soldiers in the room. The soldiers were armed, and the Jewish leaders knew full well what they could do to them if they decided to or were ordered to.

Longinus spoke. "How good of you to come and grace us with your presence. I believe you came for these," and he extended the packaged robes.

A sturdy distinguished man stepped forward to receive the robes.

"Who are you?" queried Longinus. "You aren't the high priest."

"Quite true, centurion," responded the man. "My name is Malchus. I am a servant of the high priest, the honorable Caiaphas. He has sent me to receive the robes."

"Perhaps you didn't understand," responded Longinus with an edge of anger in his voice as he fixed his eyes on Malchus. "Let me try again. I will give these robes *only* to the high priest himself. Not to anyone else under any circumstances. Is that clear? So if Caiaphas wants them, *he* can come here and claim them from me. Now, be a good servant and go tell that to your high priest."

The Centurion

Malchus blanched at the steely glare of the centurion. For a moment, he stood speechless, but the look on his face revealed that he was not pleased. The bulging of the veins in his neck revealed the rise of his anger.

"I shall inform Caiaphas," Malchus responded with a slight bow as he turned back to the delegation of priests and servants from the temple. After they had conferred for a few moments, a tall, dignified-looking man stepped forward through the group. "I am Caiaphas," he said in a resonant voice. "And I shall receive the robes now. Simeon, one of my priests, will receive them on my behalf."

Longinus recognized Caiaphas. He had not noticed him earlier because Caiaphas had kept himself hidden at the rear of group that came for the robes. Clearly, he had wanted to make this a test.

"I think not," Longinus responded, his eyes boring into the high priest. "Let me repeat what I said before: I give them to you only—not to anyone else."

An awkward silence filled the room as everyone wondered what would happen next.

After a moment's hesitation, Longinus executed a perfect about-face and began to walk resolutely out of the room into the inner recesses of the Antonia Tower, still holding the robes.

"Wait, centurion!" boomed the voice of the high priest. "I will receive the robes from you."

Longinus stopped, turned slowly, and faced the high priest. "Come then and get the robes," he ordered. "Be sure they're returned to me personally at the end of the last day of the festival. If they are not returned by my deadline, I shall dispatch a detachment of soldiers to the temple to fetch them."

The priests and their servants all gasped simultaneously, as if someone had thrown ice water on them. They certainly didn't want a band of pagan soldiers roaming around the temple, looking for the robes.

Longinus held the robes out at arm's length. It was absolutely clear he wasn't going to take them to the high priest. If Caiaphas wanted the robes, he would have to come to Longinus to get them. He would have to come like a truant to his teacher. The soldiers in the guardroom grinned as the priests grimaced.

As the high priest stepped forward to receive the robes, Longinus took a step backward and brought the robes to his chest.

Caiaphas's eyes went wide in shock and then narrowed in anger.

"Sign for them first," said Longinus coolly, "and then you may have them."

"Sign? Sign for them? I've never had to do that before!"

"That was before. This is now. Sign—and the garments are yours to wear until you return them as ordered."

"But—"

"When you return the robes, I will sign a statement acknowledging that fact," Longinus said, cutting off Caiaphas. "Then there will be no question about the transfer of the robes either way."

"I will talk to Pilate about this!" hissed the red-faced Caiaphas.

"Fine. It was his idea in the first place."

It really was Longinus's idea, but Longinus knew that Pilate would back him up because there was no love lost between Pilate and Caiaphas. Besides, when Longinus spoke officially, he spoke with the authority of Pilate, so in a way, he had told the truth, or at least enough of it to suit his purposes.

After a brief hesitation, Caiaphas capitulated: "What must I sign? Let's be done with it. I have important things to attend to." His eyes blazed with hostility, his voice dripped with acidic disdain, and his reference to other, "important things" was a deliberate slap at Longinus.

The centurion didn't respond. He had fully intended to offend the priests and their helpers. He was still wearing sandals that bore the hobnail pattern he had designed more than twenty years before—a man kneeling, begging for mercy. The message was still the same: "Mercy from me? I'll show you no mercy. I'll walk on you!"

A sullen silence pervaded the room as Caiaphas and two witnesses signed the vellum page as Longinus instructed them to do. Then Caiaphas approached Longinus, the centurion passed the robes to him, and the group of priests left in stone-cold silence. They dared not speak their feelings. Their displeasure was obvious. Even a child could have read the anger and bitterness boiling in their eyes.

As the priests left the fortress, the soldiers broke into laughter. Longinus grinned back at them and gave a thumbs-up. Along with the robes, he had delivered the message he intended to—bluntly and clearly: "Centurions are *always* in charge. Rome is always in charge. If you're not a Roman, you're dirt. Romans don't bow to you; you bow to us. We don't come to you; you come to us. We are superior; you are inferior."

Longinus felt secure, even smug. *Better to be a conqueror than to be conquered,* he mused. *Yes, much better!*

Questions for Thought and Discussion

1. The Romans hated the Jews, and the Jews hated the Romans. Where do you see prejudice and hate today? What can you, as a Christian, do to reduce prejudice and hate?

2. Both the high priest and Longinus had strong egos. Is having a strong ego a good or bad thing? Explain. When a war of egos takes place, what usually happens? When have you seen massive egos collide? What were the results?

3. In this chapter, several people suffered put-downs. Have you experienced a put-down? What happened to your emotions? How do put-downs affect relationships? What effect do they have on people's spiritual walk?

4. Caiaphas needed the robes of his office to function, and others held them. What do you need in order to function in your job, work, or home? Who holds what you need? How can you get—in positive ways that build relationships—what you need to be successful?

5. Do you find it hard or easy to ask for what you need? Why?

6. What preparations are you making now for the great festival when Jesus returns? How can you help others be ready?

Chapter 15

THE VISIT

Pilate wouldn't arrive for a few days yet, so when Longinus had completed the task of getting the high priest's garments to Caiaphas, he could spend a day or two with Julius and Livia. Once Pilate arrived, his duties would keep him at Pilate's residence in Jerusalem. But till then, he was free to use his time as he pleased—as long as all the necessary preparations were made before Pilate arrived. And, of course, even more important than seeing his friends, he wanted to see Julia again. She'd already been in Jerusalem for a few weeks.

Julius and Livia lived in a luxurious villa not far from the palace reserved for Pilate when he made official visits to Jerusalem. Now that Julius was the *chiliarch*— the leader of the thousand-plus troops in Jerusalem—his living quarters needed to reflect his status. And they certainly did.

The smooth, cool, white-marble floors accented the graceful archways and fluted, cream-colored stone columns holding up the carved-cedar ceilings.

In their villa, the guest area alone was larger than most Roman homes. It had two separate sleeping areas, a kitchen, and a large sitting room with a huge table and leather-and-wood chairs. The room was designed for both formal meetings and casual relaxation. A bubbling fountain graced one entrance to the room. At the other end stood two life-sized bronze statues of Caesar flanked by potted palm trees. Tapestries in bright red, blue, and purple hung on the walls gave a feeling of elegant warmth to the room.

Best of all, or so Longinus thought, was the private bathing area—with its three small pools, each about ten feet in diameter. As in the large public Roman baths, the pools ranged from very hot, to medium, to cool. Unlike the public baths, this area was richly adorned with plants, marble statues of the emperors, and white marble benches with matching small tables where guests could snack, relax, or read. Luxuriously soft towels were stacked at each end of the marble benches for guests to use. Adding to the comfort, the marble-tiled floor was raised on pillars so it could be warmed by fires outside the room.

"If this is how your guests live, you certainly must have quarters fit for a king, my friend!" Longinus commented as Julius showed him through the guest quarters while they waited for Julia and Livia. The two women had gone to the marketplace for the afternoon.

"This is indeed much better than the villa we had in Capernaum," replied Julius, "although that was a nice villa, too. However, I know that Pilate's personal commander doesn't live in a hovel either," Julius said with a smile.

"True enough," Longinus replied, laughing. "Pilate has treated us well. Our lodging in Caesarea is very nice. Pilate has certainly kept his promise to both of us, hasn't he?"

"Ah, yes—better than either of us could ever have dreamed of when we were back in basic training with that tough old Aquinas," responded Julius.

"You know," Longinus said. "I still remember what he taught us and even much of what he said."

"Me too," agreed Julius. "I feared him more than death itself when he was our teacher."

"I've lost track of him. Do you know what ever became of him?" queried Longinus.

"In fact, I do. He served in Spain and retired to Philippi last year. He did a bit of a tour on his way there and came through Capernaum just before we moved here," replied Julius.

"Philippi! Really? I'll have to look him up sometime when I go there with Pilate. I value what he taught us. I'd like to tell him that face to face," responded Longinus.

"What was it you said he told you? Something about decision-making?"

" 'Listen to your heart—pay attention to the inner core of who you are. Trust what you hear there, and you'll know what's right,' " repeated Longinus, remembering the words of his former master-at-arms. "I remember that saying well. In fact, it has become a kind of motto for me. It's been a solid anchor for my personal and professional life from then until now. But . . ."

"But what?" asked Julius, placing his hand on Longinus's shoulder.

"I haven't discussed this even with Julia, but things just haven't been the same since Gaius's death. How can I listen to my heart when it still hurts so much?

"And my 'inner core'? Well, I just don't know, Julius. Things aren't the same. I have a great assignment and more rank, authority, and pay than I ever imagined. I'm extremely happy with Julia and our marriage. But Gaius's death has left a hole in my inner core. A gnawing, hungry, void. A bleeding, ragged wound that hurts but doesn't heal. I'm looking for answers, but I don't seem to be able even to get the questions right," Longinus said, shaking his head.

"I hope the time off after this Passover detail will give me time to sort out some of what's going on inside me. Julia wants us to take a break—to go away for a while. She thinks that will give us a new beginning. I think she's right. I know that I certainly need it.

"You know, Julius, retirement isn't so far down the road for either of us. Julia and I need to discuss that, as well. Soldiering is all I've done for my entire adult life. I don't know what I'll do if I'm not a soldier."

"I know Gaius's death was a real blow to you," responded Julius. "He was like a son to me too."

"He had so much going for him, Julius: Julia's good looks and her sharp mind—his death just seems such a waste. He was just eighteen . . ."

Julius had no words to say. All he could do was leave his hand on Longinus's shoulder and listen as his friend poured out his heart.

"You know," Longinus said after a pause, "Julia wanted me to send for that rabbi who healed Pulcher. I refused, of course. Marcellus reported that he's a madman, so most of the time I'm glad I didn't send for him. But sometimes I wonder what if . . ."

Longinus's voice trailed off and he gazed out the portico at the puffy white clouds and bright-blue sky as if he might find an answer there. Then he continued, "Tell me, Julius, about this healing and about Pulcher. What happened?"

"You heard, of course, that Pulcher was seriously wounded in a skirmish in Apollonia in Cyrenaica—North Africa."

"Yes, I had heard that, and also that he had been put out of the legions because of those injuries."

"True," continued Julius. "I knew that he had no family, no relatives, and no place to go. So I took him in as a servant when I was assigned to Capernaum. He has changed a lot since we knew him back in basic training."

"I certainly hope so," Longinus replied with a smile. "He was a real burr under my saddle then!"

"How well I remember!" Julius said with a laugh. "But we all change over time, Longinus, and Pulcher became one of my most trusted staff, believe it or not. He really mellowed and developed. In fact, when we left Capernaum, the new commander begged me to let Pulcher stay as his household administrator."

"Remarkable! I didn't see any potential in him," said Longinus. "So what about his sickness, and healing, and the rabbi, and . . ."

"Let's sit down, and I'll tell you about it," answered Julius. "Our wives haven't returned yet, so we have some time." The two men made their way to a comfortable sitting area.

"Pulcher was working in our villa at the time. I went in to see how the household inventory was going and noticed that he didn't look at all well. He was sweating and pale. I asked him how he was feeling, and he mumbled something unintelligible. It was obvious that he was seriously ill. We put him in bed and called for a physician. He attended him for three days, but Pulcher got worse by the day. Finally, the doctor told us there was nothing more he could do."

"That sounds all too familiar," said Longinus. "So what then?"

"To tell you the truth, I didn't know what to do, so I prayed."

"Prayed? To the emperor? To your household gods? To whom did you pray?"

"To none of them," said Julius.

"To Mithra then?"

"No, to the God of the Hebrews, Yahweh."

"But you . . . But we are Romans! Why would you pray to a non-Roman god?" probed Longinus.

"Because, my friend, Yahweh is not just the God of the Jews, although they think so. He is the Creator God of all humanity—the God of the Romans too."

"How in the name of the Roman Empire did you ever arrive at that opinion?" asked Longinus.

"When I learned that Pilate was posting me to Capernaum with a follow-up assignment to Jerusalem, I began to read some of the scrolls of the Hebrews. I needed to understand the people Rome wanted me to govern. What I found astonished me, thrilled me, and changed me. As a result, I began to give funds to build the synagogue in Capernaum."

"I heard about that. I wondered what was going on when you, a Roman centurion, gave your hard-earned silver to build a Jewish house of worship," interrupted Longinus.

"It's not just a house of Jewish worship, Longinus—it is a house of worship for all people. Even for us Romans. I read in the proverbs of Solomon, in one of the scrolls, 'He who is kind to the poor lends to God, and He will reward him for what he has done.' So I decided to make a 'loan' to help build the synagogue. Livia and I have no children; we are well paid by Rome, so why not help out with the synagogue and other needs?"

"What does this have to do with Pulcher? I'm lost."

"Well, when the synagogue was finished and in regular use, a new rabbi who is filled with fresh ideas visited the synagogue often. I heard him teach on several occasions and recognized his teachings to be accurate reflections of the scrolls I was reading. Some of his own kinsmen were quite upset at what he said and taught, but he touched and changed me.

"I heard that he not only taught good lessons on living but that he had power to do miracles. And that's what the doctor said Pulcher needed—a miracle."

"Go on," invited Longinus.

"So when I heard that the teacher was entering town, I went to him personally and told him that my servant was ill at home, paralyzed and suffering greatly. The teacher offered to come to my house and heal Pulcher."

"He offered to come to your house? How unusual! Rabbis don't volunteer to enter a Roman house! Most of them would shun us like death," Longinus commented aloud. He couldn't help thinking about his recent interaction with the high priest and his people.

Julius continued, "I told him, 'Sir, I don't deserve to have you come under my roof. All you need to do is say the word and he will be healed. I understand authority, and I believe in your authority.'

"The teacher surprised me. He told the crowd that I had more faith than 'the chosen'—as the Jews call themselves. Then he added that my request was honored! He said God had seen my good deeds and had granted my request for Pulcher. That very afternoon, Pulcher's paralysis left. By evening, he was fully recovered."

"I'm stunned!" Longinus said. "What you've told me seems impossible! If I'd heard this from anyone but you, Julius, I wouldn't have believed it. But I know you to be honest. And you say the rabbi Jesus made him well?"

"Yes, Jesus—Jesus of Nazareth."

Longinus's brow wrinkled in concern. He said, "Jesus of Nazareth. Marcellus Sylvanus says he's a madman, and you tell me that he works miracles. Something doesn't fit. I'm very confused!"

"Remember what old Aquinas told us," said Julius with a smile. "Listen to your heart—pay attention to the inner core of who you are. Trust what you hear there, and you will know what's right."

Longinus could hear the cadence of Aquinas's words as Julius repeated them. *Julius seems to have found some answers,* Longinus thought to himself. *Perhaps I will too, but right now it's a puzzle to me. This teacher, this Jesus—I wonder what kind of person he is? Maybe someday I'll meet him. If anyone other than Julius had told me this story, I would have thought he had too much wine. But I know Julius, and I trust him.*

Out loud he said, "Thanks for telling me about Pulcher, Julius. It's very interesting. I'll have to give it more thought. For now, let's get something to eat. I'm hungry!"

Questions for Thought and Discussion

1. When have you felt the need for a new beginning? What issues prompted that need? What did you do about it?

2. When Longinus confided in Julius about his ongoing deep grief at the loss of Gaius, Julius just listened. Who will listen to you in your time of need? To whom do you need to listen?

3. Julius not only listened but he touched Longinus. Is touch important when dealing with deep issues, or is it a distraction? When has touch

been important and healing for you? What are some boundary issues about touching others?

4. Julius saw some redeeming qualities beneath the rough exterior of Pulcher and took him in when he had needs. When have you either seen or missed deeper qualities in others? Recall some biblical accounts of God seeing through tough exteriors to the positive potential in people. How has God done that for you?

5. Julius saw the Capernaum synagogue as a place of worship for all people, including himself. How inclusive is your congregation? How inclusive are you?

6. Julius simply shared with Longinus what Jesus had done in his life: no pressure, no demands, no pushing. How effective is that kind of witnessing? What has Jesus done in your life that you can share with friends?

Chapter 16

THE STAGE IS SET

Julia and Livia had a great time together in Jerusalem. The shops, the hustle and bustle of traders from all over selling all manner of goods, was exciting. Adding to that activity were the pilgrims who came for the Passover Feast. The combination added dashes of spice and energy to the throngs of people gathering for the Passover event. The two women were sure this would be a memorable time.

Their husbands had their hands full with preparations to receive Pilate and Claudia. Security was extremely tight because tensions were high. A young Roman soldier had wandered into the back streets of the city and had been caught by a group of extremely radical zealots, *sacarri*—those with curved knives. They had murdered him and dumped his body, leaving a note with it that said, "This is what we will do to any Roman who dares enter Jerusalem, the Holy City."

Julius's forces quickly rounded up all known and suspected zealots and soon brought charges against one of the ringleaders—a brigand known as Barabbas. His name meant "son of the father." The Roman soldiers called him a "son of . . ." and concluded the phrase with several unsavory terms. Roman justice would be swift and brutal for him. He was to be made a public example—he would be crucified between two thieves to show what would happen to anyone who dared to harm a Roman or who thought of trying to stir up trouble during the Passover celebrations. Rome would tolerate Jewish holy events but not troublemakers. The crucifixion was scheduled for Friday just outside the city walls, where all the pilgrims could view it.

Pilate and Claudia were safe and comfortable in their quarters, and Longinus had planned to stay with his soldiers and Pilate until the Passover celebrations were finished. Julia understood that she would be an operational widow during that time. "Mission first," Longinus had told her. It was language she understood well, having lived with a soldier for so many years. In fact, she had told her father many times, "I'm married to the man, but I'm also married to the military."

Julia had learned to accept the realities of being the wife of a career military man. She had also learned to let Longinus's absence build anticipation for their time away together when his responsibilities ended. In fact, she had purchased a new robe and perfumed oil with which she would celebrate the respite from the rigors of command. As she told Livia with a smile, "We need a new beginning, and that's just around the corner for us. It'll be great!"

Thursday night, about *primafax*—the time to light the lamps—a runner came to Longinus, informing him that a delegation from the temple had arrived seeking a contingent of Roman soldiers to "help them apprehend a serious troublemaker." *That's odd,* thought Longinus. *Usually, the Jews want absolutely nothing to do with the Romans, so why this sudden cooperation? And why is this happening now, on the verge of the Passover?* His suspicions were aroused, just as they would have been were he marching into battle. Early in his military career, he had learned that "when things don't add up, caution is the best road to take." That aphorism certainly seemed appropriate now.

"Sir," suggested the *optio,* Marcus, "perhaps they're beginning to understand that working with us rather than against us is in their own best interests."

"Well spoken, Marcus. We can indeed hope that's the case. Take a detachment of soldiers, go with them, and report back to me when the task is done," ordered Longinus.

"As you command, sir!" replied Marcus with a sharp salute. Longinus smiled. Marcus was a good soldier. He was apt, loyal, and always eager to serve. Longinus had concluded that Marcus had what it took to become a centurion, and he had determined to do what he could to advance his career. Serving with Pilate's elite troops would certainly help his career even as it enhanced Longinus's.

The Centurion

Longinus made a last sweep of his subordinate commanders and troops before retiring to his cot for the night. He would much rather be in Julius's guest quarters with Julia, but duty demanded his presence in the stark barracks rather than the luxurious guest quarters. Julia would just have to enjoy them by herself. So, Longinus drifted off to sleep and dreamed of Julia. Dreams would have to suffice for a few more days.

Well before the cock-crowing at the first hour of the day, Longinus was up and moving. He had armored up and taken breakfast in the predawn darkness with his soldiers in the troops' galley. As the meal was ending, Marcus came in to report what had happened during the night assignment. Longinus knew immediately that something was wrong. Marcus, usually relaxed and outgoing, appeared to be as taut as a bowstring in battle.

"Sir, I need to make my report to you in private, if it is possible, sir." Though Marcus spoke quietly, his tone was urgent.

"Of course," Longinus replied. "Step into the command quarters. We can talk privately there."

As soon as they were away from the eyes and ears of the other soldiers, Marcus began to report what had happened. The words spilled out of him like water over a rock dam—his words tumbled over each other as if competing to be expressed. "Sir, I've never seen anything like it. . . . The crowds . . . the shouting . . . we all fell back . . . the fisherman's knife . . ."

"Slow down. Collect yourself," Longinus said, his concern showing in his voice. "Take a deep breath, start over, and tell me what happened, Marcus."

"Sir, it's hard to know where to begin," stammered the young *optio.*

"Begin with when you left here last night."

"Yes, sir. I did as you said, sir. I got a detachment of soldiers and went with the temple guards on their mission to capture this 'troublemaker.' I thought that we would be looking for someone else who was with that murderer Barabbas. But the Jewish authorities had a different mission in mind.

"We went to the temple complex and waited until the first watch after midnight. Then, a furtive man came to lead us to the one we were to arrest. It was clear this man had a thorough knowledge of who our quarry was and where we would find him. He was a rather sullen follow and was obviously paid to be an informant. I saw him accept a bag that jingled as if it contained coins from the priests, and I heard somebody whisper that he was a traitor. That only heightened my concerns that we might be walking into a trap."

"Go on," Longinus instructed.

"We went across the Kidron Brook and into a grove of olive trees. In the trees, our torches cast deep shadows that made it difficult to see. The clouds that occasionally passed in front of the moon added to the spooky atmosphere of the place. Suddenly, in the mist, I saw a single figure. He looked . . ." Marcus stopped, searching for words.

"He looked?"

"He . . . he looked . . . like he had blood all over his face . . . like he had been in some ghastly battle. I tell you, sir, it was unnerving. He asked us who we were looking for. The temple guards didn't recognize him, but the fellow who brought us there—Judas was his name—recognized the man in the mist, and he embraced him and kissed him on the cheek.

"Then . . . I can't explain it. . . . There was a kind of explosion or—"

"Explosion?"

"Well, not exactly an explosion because there was no sound. There was a burst of light or lightning or something that flashed so brightly that we all stumbled back. All except this Judas fellow. As I say, he embraced and kissed the man in greeting. I guess it was his way of showing us that we could touch the man too.

"Then there was utter confusion. A small band of people rushed out of the trees and darkness. One of them was screaming and swinging a knife. I thought we'd walked into an ambush and that the Jews would turn on me and our troops and slaughter us all. But they didn't.

"I had seized the prisoner and immediately tied his hands, just as you taught me to do, sir—wrists crossed, loops around the wrists, and then secured with three twists around the ropes between his wrists.

"I looked up and saw the guy with the knife take a swing at the high priest's servant—that Malchus fellow who was here the other day to get the robes. Malchus saw the knife coming and spun violently to one side to escape the blow. He almost made it."

"Almost?" asked Longinus.

"Yes, sir, almost—but not fully. The next thing I knew, Malchus was screaming and holding the right side of his head and blood was streaming through his fingers and running down his face and neck. The attacker turned and ran away, leaving Malchus howling like a wounded wolf. I saw that the attacker had cut off Malchus's right ear—cut it off completely, as clean as a butcher trims a piece of roast.

"At that point everything came to a halt and there was an eerie silence. Then . . . then . . . oh, then . . ."

"Then what, Marcus? Speak up!" encouraged Longinus.

"Sir, I *know* I had tied his hands tightly, just as you taught me. It always secures our prisoners. I've done it hundreds of times, but . . ."

"But what?" pressed Longinus.

"But the prisoner's hands were suddenly free, as if the ropes were mere shadows, and then . . ." Marcus's voice trailed off as his eyes widened.

"Then?" Longinus demanded.

"The prisoner bent over, picked up the severed ear, and . . ." and Marcus's voice trailed off into a whisper, "I saw him. I saw him do it!"

"You saw him do what?"

"I saw him put the ear back in place on Malchus, sir. He just picked the ear up from the ground and put it back on Malchus's head. He put it back, and it stayed as if it had never been cut off. I swear by all the gods of Rome that I saw it with my own eyes. It really happened, sir. Just as I said."

"And then?"

"Then this prisoner said that he was the one we wanted so we should let the men who were with him go. There was no problem with that! One fellow ran right out of his tunic and disappeared into the darkness stark naked.

"It was so strange. The prisoner turned to me and held out his hands so I could retie them. I have to tell you, sir, I was scared even to touch him, let alone bind his hands again. He looked me in the eyes and said, 'Don't be afraid. It has to be this way.' Malchus just stood there touching his ear with his mouth wide open and his eyes bulging. As for me, sir, I could hear my heart pounding so hard that I thought it would jump completely out of my armor."

"What happened then?" urged Longinus. "That was six hours ago. What else happened? I'll have to give a full report to Pilate."

"Yes, sir, I know. We took the prisoner to the house of Annas, the former high priest—Caiaphas's father-in-law. There was some kind of inquiry or judgment going on. The Jewish temple guards were roughing up the prisoner. I sent our men to intervene.

"After that, we marched the prisoner to the house of Caiaphas, where they had another kind of court hearing. They put him in a dungeon and were allowing the temple guards and rabble to beat him freely. I sent our troops in again to restore order. The mob was insane. They were demonic, shrieking at him, spitting on him, hitting and kicking him. When they calmed down, some other groups came in about sunrise at the cock-crowing, and they conducted another trial. Suddenly, they started screaming that he should die and began to beat him again."

"By the mercies of Mithra, what kind of renegade is this man that his own people would be so vicious to him?" asked Longinus.

"I don't know. But we intervened again, or they would have killed him on the spot. I made the call to stop it because I was afraid his death would ignite a riot across the whole of Jerusalem. One thing is for sure, there was enough hate there to fuel a war."

"You did the right thing, Marcus. So where is the prisoner now?"

"He's just outside. I had no other choice. I declared him to be a prisoner of Rome. We'll have to hold him until the matter can be settled. I guess His Excellency, Pilate, will have to deal with him."

"I suppose so. Pilate will be less than thrilled with the task, but it's better than letting a citywide riot break out. That would have pleased him even less and undoubtedly would have cost many lives. Good job, Marcus. You will be rewarded for your courage and diligence," Longinus said.

"May I be dismissed, sir? My nerves feel as if they've been scrubbed with gravel and salt. I could use a break, if you please, sir."

"Of course, Marcus. You're dismissed. Oh, one more thing."

"Yes, sir?"

"The prisoner. Who is he? What's his name? Pilate will need to know."

"His name is Jesus. Jesus of Nazareth, sir."

Questions for Thought and Discussion

1. Julia called herself an "operational widow" because Longinus would be

focused on his job, not on her. Does that happen in your family? How frequently? What are the results? What can you do to keep your job from siphoning life out of your personal or spiritual relationships?

2. Longinus said, "When things don't add up, caution is the best road to take." Do you agree or disagree? Where is the line between caution and paranoia?

3. What Marcus expected to happen and what actually happened were vastly different. When has that been your experience? What was the event? How did you handle it? How did it affect you?

4. Put yourself in Marcus's sandals. What would it be like for you to have witnessed Jesus' healing of Malchus? Have you seen or experienced a miracle? If so, how did it affect you?

5. Marcus feared he was walking into an ambush. When have you felt that you were walking into an ambush emotionally, spiritually, or physically? What were your feelings, your actions, and the outcome?

6. After seeing Jesus heal Malchus, Marcus was afraid to tie Jesus' hands. Why do you think some people are afraid of God? If you have been afraid of God, what was going on at the time? How can you help someone who fears God to develop trust in Him?

Chapter 17

BEFORE PILATE

Jesus of Nazareth!

The words hit Longinus like a bolt of lightning. Could this be the same one who healed Pulcher? The one Marcus reported had healed a severed ear and who had nearly caused one of Longinus's best young officers to come unglued like a shield left out in the rain? Could this be the man Marcellus had spied on and whom he concluded "is a madman"?

Now, this Jesus had been dragged in bonds to the Antonia Tower overlooking the temple complex by a motley mob demanding that Pilate judge him. Longinus could hear the rough voices, the shrill shouts, and the frenzied crowd even as he approached the arched stone portico and the six-inch-thick wooden gates that barred entrance to the tower. When he stepped into the morning light, his armor reflected the early rays of the sun like flashes of blood-colored lightning.

The cacophony dimmed as if silenced by a huge blanket, and all eyes turned toward him. His helmet, sword, and demeanor were ample announcements of his rank. No one—not even those who had little contact with the Roman military—could miss the fact that he was a very senior centurion and that disrespecting him could bring a swift and deadly response.

"What do you want?" barked Longinus roughly.

"We have brought this man to be judged by Pilate," said one of the priests. "He is a rebel and an insurrectionist. We want peace during the holy days of the

135

sacred Passover, but this man wants trouble. So we have brought him to Pilate."

That's a new day—or an outright lie, Longinus thought to himself. *These people never want to cooperate with Rome. They would rather dance with the devil than be helpful to Rome.*

"You've come too early in the morning," challenged Longinus.

"We know it's early, but we also know that Pilate will have a full day and that he reserves the early mornings for audience with his loyal subjects who have urgent matters to settle."

Part of the statement was indeed true. Scheduled meetings and other official duties would consume the later parts of the day and often stretch long into the night. So, like other Roman officials, Pilate kept the hours just after dawn open for anyone who wished to have an audience with him. The part of the statement about the mob being "loyal subjects" was a barefaced lie. They knew it, and Longinus knew it as well.

Longinus had long ago learned to trust his instincts in situations like this, and his instincts told him that this scenario was all wrong. While he didn't know the details, he was keenly aware that the pieces didn't fit together.

"So?" Longinus said.

"Since this is the Day of Preparation," answered another priest, "we can't enter Pilate's court. But we respectfully request that His Honor Pilate come out here to judge this troublemaker."

Just then, Longinus caught his first glimpse of Jesus, who stood surrounded by a knot of agitated temple guards and religious officials. He had been severely beaten. Blood trickled in a bright-red ribbon from the corner of his mouth. His nose appeared to be severely swollen. His eyes were starting to swell shut, and the yellow-greenish cast below his right eye would soon be purple with bruising and swelling.

Jesus appeared to be bound, although he wasn't resisting his captors, nor did he look as if he would attempt to get away. The chains were calculated to make a statement about the man—to impress Pilate that he was dangerous and should be treated like some lowlife.

So, this is Jesus, thought Longinus, *the one many revere, and who some—like this crowd—revile.*

As Longinus looked at Jesus more closely, trying to discern if he would or could offer any physical threat to Pilate, he was struck by the calm, dignified bearing of the man. Longinus thought, *He would make a good soldier—a good leader.* Jesus didn't appear to be intimidated in the least by the people hounding him. He looked as if he were in charge, not in chains.

Longinus had seen many criminals. By the time they were brought to him, they tended to be hardened, sullen, and desperate. Their angry demeanor or, in some cases, their abject groveling for mercy, revealed their characters. But this man showed neither reaction. He was the only calm one in the frenzied crowd. He stood erect, but not haughty. His gaze was clear and penetrating. Longinus could see why the man had so shaken Marcus.

Who is this man? Longinus found himself asking. *He has changed Marcus, reportedly done a miracle to heal Malchus, and managed to enrage the temple leaders, upsetting his own people to the point of their coming here to talk with Pilate.*

"Well, centurion, are you going to get Pilate?" someone in the crowd yelled.

The insolent question—almost an order—caught Longinus off guard. He wasn't used to being addressed like a schoolboy. Both his rank and his bearing called for deference, not defiance. He chose not to respond, ignoring the shout as if it were a piece of camel-hair fluff floating in the breeze.

"What is the charge you bring against this man? I won't go to Pilate with an empty slate, so either state your business clearly or be gone before I release the cohort on you," challenged Longinus.

"He's a troublemaker!" shouted someone.

"He's a threat to peace," shouted another.

Longinus smiled inwardly as the suggestion that this Jesus was a troublemaker. He may have been a troublemaker, but not for Rome. He seemed to have stirred up trouble from the religious leaders and their supporters. Perhaps he was a threat to their egos. He didn't appear to be a threat to Rome.

The anger of the crowd grew, threatening to overwhelm their collective judgment. It was clear to Longinus that a riot could be in the making. No need for that. He held up his hand for silence. "I will consult with Pilate," he said. "He may or may not hear you. But you hear this: if you cause any trouble here this morning, I will order my troops to deal with you immediately and fully. Is that clear?"

The crowd murmured quietly but angrily. The looks on their faces spoke of sheer hatred.

"Is that clear?" demanded Longinus.

"Yes, it is clear, centurion," responded one of the priests.

"Good. I shall consult with Pilate and return. If, when I return, there is any disturbance, you shall meet some of my best soldiers up very close and intimately."

The looks on the faces in the crowd told Longinus that his message had hit the mark like the armor-piercing *pila* spears that his soldiers brandished. There would be no riot from this group, or they would wind up skewered like pieces of lamb.

Longinus went into the Antonia Tower, where Pilate was washing his hands and face in a bronze basin in preparation for the day's activities. He had already put on his white linen robe and the elaborate toga that identified him as the procurator and representative of Rome.

Pilate said, "Good morning, Longinus. The look on your face suggests that my day may begin early but not nicely. Is that correct?"

Pilate's long tenure in the legions and his work with people had taught him how to read both people and situations rapidly and accurately.

"Yes, sir, you are correct on both counts—unfortunately."

Pilate smiled, pleased with himself. "I suspected that my presence in Jerusalem during the Passover time would be filled with, shall we say, exciting opportunities to excel."

The comment brought a slight smile to Longinus's face, too.

"Well, what exciting news do you bring from the rabble of the community?"

"Sir, there is a delegation—make that a crowd—of temple leaders who have brought someone to be judged by you. I suspect they are up to something, but I haven't quite figured out what. I have observed the man they brought, and I believe he is no threat to you or to Rome. I suspect the dispute is an internal affair, but they are asking you to judge him."

"Ah, yes. These people can cause more trouble over nothing than any others in the empire. Do you recall the agitation that came because of my bringing standards bearing the likeness of the emperor into the tower? By the eyes of the gods, the standards were in *our* space, not theirs, but they pitched a fit anyway," Pilate said.

"Yes, sir. That was before I joined you, but I do recall hearing about the incident. You handled it well, as I recall."

"Thank you, Longinus. I do try to govern these people, but it isn't easy or pleasant. They always seem to have complaints about something," remarked Pilate, as he carefully folded his towel and placed it on the marble stand by the basin.

"So what is the charge they bring, and who is the fellow they want me to judge?"

Longinus was prepared to answer both questions. He had served Pilate long enough to know what information Pilate would ask for.

"They didn't specify a charge other than to say he is a troublemaker, and they claim to want to cooperate with us in dealing with him."

That brought a frown to Pilate's face. "They want to *cooperate* with us! That would be the day silver *denarii* rained from the clouds, and the rivers would run rich with wine! Something doesn't fit."

"My thoughts too, sir," opined Longinus. "And they say they can't bring the man into the tower for your judgment because they want to stay ceremonially clean for Passover, I believe."

"I anticipated that. I try to study up on the customs of the people, and this would be in keeping with their practices, although they seem to be able to bend the rules when they want to do so for their own benefit or convenience. I suppose they want me to come to them?"

"Yes, sir, that is their request, although they made it sound more like a demand," offered Longinus.

"Very well," sighed Pilate. "Let's get on with it. Have your soldiers move my chair out onto the balcony, where I can speak with them and try to see what is bothering them this time."

"Consider it done, sir," said Longinus, as he gave a smart salute.

When the chair was in place, Pilate strode out onto the balcony and seated himself. As he did, the crowd began to shout and wave their arms.

Longinus stepped to the balustrade and motioned for the people to be quiet. "You wished to confer with the procurator. Here he is. But, as I told you earlier, we will not allow this to get out of hand. Quiet down, and then tell Pilate what your needs are."

Pilate asked, "What charge do you bring against this man?"

The Centurion

At that, the crowd began to roar. "If he weren't an evildoer, we wouldn't have brought him to you," was the gist of what they were saying.

Pilate looked intently at the prisoner. He had heard reports about this man and had hoped to see him sometime. As he scrutinized Jesus, he was struck by the same qualities Longinus had seen earlier. Jesus was an island of calm in a sea of tempestuous unrest. His bearing was regal, his demeanor serene, even though it was obvious to Pilate that he had been severely beaten.

It was just as obvious to Pilate that the crowd was intent on taking this man's life. They were here because only the Romans could mete out the death sentence. While Pilate had little or no sympathy for anyone, including the prisoner before him this bright morning, he also knew how much the crowd wanted him to comply with their request. This gave him reason to resist them. It was a kind of cat-and-mouse game, and Pilate enjoyed irritating them by refusing their demands.

Pilate thought for a moment, then waved his hand dismissively and said, "Judge him yourselves," and turned to walk back into the Antonia Tower.

The people were stunned by his quick dismissal. A collective gasp arose from the crowd, and then they roared, "We can't condemn him to death, but you should. He has called himself a king and perverted the people, telling them not to pay taxes."

With that, Pilate turned and waved for Longinus to bring the prisoner to him for examination.

"Are you a king?" Pilate asked, smiling with disdain as he spoke to Jesus.

"Did you discover that for yourself or did someone tell you that?" Jesus responded evenly.

"Am I a Jew that I would know these things?" snorted Pilate.

"For this I was born into the world," replied Jesus. Then he added, "You would have no authority over me if it were not given to you from above. I tell you the truth, I am a king."

"Truth! What is truth?" Pilate shot back angrily.

Perhaps Pilate read into Jesus' reply a slap at his being procurator only because it was a gift from Tiberius, Longinus thought. The more Longinus evaluated Jesus' response though, the more it seemed that Jesus was talking about an authority well above that of either Pilate or Tiberius.

Pilate returned again to the crowd gathered below the balcony. "I find no fault in him," he said.

Now the crowd went wild. "He should die! He said he is the son of God!"

That caught Pilate's curiosity. He told Longinus to bring Jesus to him yet again. This time, Jesus wouldn't say a word. It was as if he were saying, "You know the truth. Nothing I can say will change that—or you. You must make your judgment based on what you already know. You're on your own."

Pilate repeated to the boiling mob what he had said before: "I find no fault in him."

"He's a troublemaker!" the crowd howled. "He's stirred up people all through Galilee!"

At that, Pilate stopped and slowly scanned the crowd. "Did you say 'Galilee'?"

"Yes, and other places too," the crowd responded, shaking their fists in the air to drive home the point.

"Is he a Galilean?"

"Yes, he is," they responded.

"Since he is a Galilean, let Herod—your Galilean king—judge him," decreed Pilate as he walked briskly back into the tower. As he strode past Longinus, he winked and said, "See to it, Longinus, and report to me what Herod does with this case."

Longinus knew that the smirk on Pilate's face meant that he knew he had thwarted the plans of the crowd by "dumping" the situation into Herod's lap. Pilate was playing with them. The relationship between Herod and him was strained and wary. Neither trusted the other. Tensions constantly arose between them over many issues. Maybe Pilate could get a double positive out of this—he could build a little bridge between himself and Herod and at the same time harass the temple leaders by not doing what they demanded. So Pilate went to his quarters to have a sumptuous breakfast with Claudia Procula while Longinus had the distasteful business of taking Jesus to Herod.

This will give me a chance to observe this man and to evaluate him, Longinus thought. His curiosity had been aroused about this Jesus; now he would have a chance to see for himself why the temple leaders were so angry and how Jesus could be so utterly calm.

Longinus sensed that this could turn out to be a very long day for him. But then, long or short, easy or gruelingly difficult, he was a soldier, and he would do what needed to be done. He gathered a small band of soldiers, and they started off toward Herod's palace. At Longinus's direction, Jesus marched in the middle of the Roman contingent. It was as much to protect him as it was to be sure he didn't escape. Now that Jesus was under his control, Longinus was responsible for him in every way. That included protection from the angry crowd as much as making sure he was delivered to Herod.

A runner was sent ahead to inform Herod that the contingent was on its way. It would not do to surprise Herod. He had a foul temper and thought he should be treated like a king even by the Romans, who allowed him to have the title.

Longinus disliked Herod as much as Pilate did, but orders were orders.

Questions for Thought and Discussion

1. Roman leaders had an open-door policy for the discussion of issues. Is that policy a good or a bad one? Why? How can you schedule time for open discussion of secular and spiritual issues?

2. Both Pilate and Longinus noticed that Jesus was calm in chaos. How do you act in chaotic situations? What can you do to increase your calmness under pressure? What kind of witness for Christ are you when you are stressed?

3. When have you seen or been part of a "crowd mentality"? What was it like? What were the issues? The actions and outcomes? Discuss some of the dangers in a crowd mentality.

4. Pilate sent Jesus to Herod. What is the difference between "dumping" and delegating? Are you a delegator or a dumper?

5. Longinus threatened to unleash his troops to quell any disturbance. What are the limits of threats when used to control situations? What limitations do threats have when used to control children? What does that approach teach people?

6. How and when do you try to avoid responsibility for decision-making? Why? How can you develop more decisiveness?

Chapter 18

TO HEROD AND BACK

Herod was a "king" only because the Romans allowed him to act in that capacity. He was from the Herodian family line—a lineage of some of the most corrupt and despotic leaders ever seen in Palestine. It was said in Roman circles that it was "better to be Herod's *hys* than his *huios*." In other words, it was better to be Herod's pig than his son.

That saying elicited raucous laughter from the Romans, who knew that Jews wouldn't touch pigs and that some of the Herods had murdered wives, children, friends, and family to stay in power.

So, Herod was a murderous thug, but the Romans allowed him to stay in power because he always paid tribute to the Romans on time. True, he took advantage of those he ruled, but that mattered little to Rome. So long as the taxes came in and there were no overt threats to their power, Herod was welcome to stay. Pig or prince—it mattered not, as long as the emperor got his due.

Longinus and his band of soldiers wound their way through the crowded streets of Jerusalem to Herod's palace, which was situated high on a hill overlooking the city. Herod had usurped the land and had built a palatial compound for his convenience whenever he was in Jerusalem. The place was walled and guarded—a mini-fortress.

The security was as much to protect Herod from his subjects—with whom he was grossly unpopular—as it was to secure the grounds from the petty thieves who abounded within the city. They were particularly pesky during the Passover season, when pilgrims from all over made excellent targets for pickpockets and others who would gladly relieve them of the gold and silver they carried to purchase animals to be sacrificed—and for the other offerings required at the temple services.

Petty thieves were a consideration, of course. Each soldier carried a side knife known as a *pugio*. Because of the blade's shape, it was not only deadly going into a body, but when turned and then withdrawn, it caused even more damage on exit. This death-dealing implement was very much sought after by thieves not only because of its deadly design but because everyone knew a soldier would never part with his fighting knife willingly. Thus, the instrument was a prize to steal from an unwary soldier. It would give bragging rights to the thief, as well as bringing a handsome price in the marketplace.

The Roman contingent arrived at Herod's palace with no incidents, probably in great part due to the procession being led by Longinus on a huge stallion. The animal had been trained to respond only to the will and command of its rider and to ignore any distracting sounds or movements intended to make it shy. It had been trained as a warhorse that would trample anyone who didn't get out of its way.

When Longinus's procession arrived at the palace, guards swung the huge, rough timber-and-iron gate open to receive Longinus and his entourage. The runner had informed Herod of the impending meeting with Jesus, and Herod was more than ready to see this man face to face.

It had been rumored that Herod was afraid of Jesus, and that he had said he feared that Jesus was the resurrected John the Baptist, whom Herod had executed only a few months before. His palace guards had tried to calm his fears by pointing out that Jesus was a relative of John the Baptist, but not the person himself.

Herod had heard about Jesus' miracle-working powers and wanted to see for himself what Jesus could and would do. So, Pilate's ploy to rid himself of the prisoner delighted Herod, for now he would have the chance to see Jesus—and in the privacy and protection of his own palace rather than in a public forum, where Jesus might embarrass or challenge him as had John the Baptist.

Because of the Passover events, Herod had gathered guests and was in the midst of throwing a feast when word came from Pilate that Jesus was being sent to him. Herod seized the opportunity to make a grand spectacle of his own kingly power in contrast with the helplessness of Jesus, who was being delivered to him as a prisoner.

Herod had several cripples brought in. When Jesus stood before Herod, the king mocked him and offered to release him if Jesus would heal the cripples for the amusement of the gathered crowd. "Perform a miracle for us, and you are a free man," he said.

Miracle? Longinus recalled in vividly sharp focus the report Marcus had given him about how Jesus had performed a miracle in restoring the ear of Malchus, the servant of the high priest. Now, Jesus was being offered freedom from torment and certain death if he would do what he apparently had the power to do.

At the mention of releasing the prisoner, Longinus involuntarily stiffened in his armor. *This man is a prisoner of Pilate and under my charge. Herod has no right or power to release him without my permission or that of Pilate,* he thought silently to himself. He waited to see how Jesus would respond to the offer of pardon. But as Herod bullied him, he made absolutely no response.

"Don't you know," ranted Herod, "that I have the authority to have you killed or to have you released?" Herod's face was twisted with rage that Jesus was ignoring him in front of all the guests—and right here in Herod's own palace at that.

Longinus was struck again with the calmness of the prisoner even when face to face with the ranting Herod. Would he free himself by doing the demanded miracle? Could he do miracles, or had Marcus merely imagined what had happened in the garden just hours before? Longinus certainly trusted Marcus more than Herod. What would this Jesus do? Longinus watched intently.

Herod demanded, begged, cajoled, and threatened. He screamed and became furious at Jesus, shaking his fists and growing red in the face with utter frustration. Jesus remained calm and didn't say a word to Herod. Nothing. He gave absolutely no acknowledgment that Herod even existed.

Again, Longinus asked himself, *Who is this man? He changes everyone with whom he comes in contact. He changed Marcus. He is changing Herod—certainly not for the better—but changing him nonetheless.*

The Centurion

Finally, in utter frustration, Herod pushed Jesus into the waiting arms of his household guards, who marched Jesus out of the banquet hall as Herod turned back to his guests, angry and beaten by Jesus' calm defiance.

Herod's guards took Jesus into the courtyard, where they began to kick and punch Jesus mercilessly. They acted out with their fists and feet what Herod had put into brutal and blunt words. Their anger burst out like a thunderstorm laden with deadly lightning. The crowd that had followed the procession to Herod's palace began to beat and mock Jesus too. The soldiers threw one of Herod's old robes over Jesus' face so he couldn't see the blows coming and dodge them. Then they beat him with forceful blows against which he had neither warning nor protection. His head snapped repeatedly to the right and then to the left.

Since Jesus was still under Roman jurisdiction, Longinus ordered his soldiers to intervene before Herod's henchmen killed him. As the Roman soldiers took the prisoner from Herod's snarling guards, Herod, who had been watching from a balcony, screamed, "Take him back to Pilate! I want nothing to do with him!"

Longinus was eager to get out of the presence of this vile king, whom many had dubbed "the Fox" because of his rabid reactions and biting cruelty. Not that Longinus and his troops couldn't handle the situation. They could have taken on the whole crowd and defeated them, but Longinus didn't want to start an "incident" that would set off riots in the streets. Too many insurrectionists and zealots were in Jerusalem just looking for trouble, just waiting for an excuse to riot. Longinus didn't want to drop a spark into that tinderbox, so back to Pilate they went with Jesus in their custody.

Pilate wasn't overjoyed to see them come back. He knew that he would now have to judge this man. The mood of the crowd before him was even more agitated and angry than before.

Pilate went out to the crowd. He bluntly reminded them that he had already said he found no fault in the man. Furthermore, he pointed out that Herod had examined him and found no fault in him either.

At that, the unruly crowd began to scream and howl like madmen. The situation was beginning to get out of control; Longinus feared that he would have to put a stop to it by dispatching his troops into the crowd. Then Longinus saw

Claudia Procula standing at the portico to Pilate's and her private quarters. She had a small scroll in her hand and motioned for Longinus to take it and deliver it to Pilate.

That's highly unusual, thought Longinus. *She doesn't usually become involved in any cases that come before Pilate.*

Longinus was sure there was no threat from Jesus, so he walked quickly to her, took the scroll, and brought it to Pilate.

Pilate was puzzled by Claudia's interruption. He opened the scroll and began to read it. Longinus looked over his shoulder to read the note, too. It was an unusual thing for him to do, but these were unusual situations, and he wanted to know in order to be able to anticipate what might come next.

Claudia had written, "Have nothing to do with this righteous man. I have suffered much in a dream about him!"

Both Pilate and Longinus were stunned. Claudia was essentially saying that the gods had sent her a dream—an omen, a warning for Pilate to leave Jesus alone. The message couldn't have been more clearly stated had it been written in blazing flames across the sky.

Now Pilate was nearly beside himself with concern. It was written all over his face and demeanor. He wanted nothing more than to rid himself of the dilemma developing before him.

Pilate had only minted three coins in his procuratorship—two of them had the *littus,* the staff of the augur, on them. He didn't put his name or face on the coins, just the symbol of omens and intervention from the gods. That is how much stock he put in augury and omens. Now his wife was telling him she had a message from the gods for him about this man the crowd was saying had called himself the son of God. Pilate's distress was palpable.

Then Longinus saw a slight smile come to Pilate's face—more a smirk than a smile. Pilate stood, raised his arms for silence, and announced, "Because of your Passover holiday and my great favors to you, I will release a prisoner to you—one of your choice. I will release either Barabbas or Jesus, your king."

Longinus was shocked at the potential injustice—but also impressed by Pilate's cunning. He was offering the crowd a choice that he thought would get him off the hook of condemning to death a man he thought innocent. They could choose either Barabbas, a murderous thug, or Jesus, a harmless rabbi who might even appeal to their nationalistic fervor as "king of the Jews." Clearly, Pilate was desperate or he would not have made the offer. *Is he afraid of this Jesus?* wondered Longinus. Obviously, Claudia Procula's note had struck a nerve.

"Release Barabbas! Release Barabbas!" the crowd howled, as though directed by an unseen conductor. "We want Barabbas!"

"Then what shall I do with Jesus?" asked Pilate.

"Crucify him," they began to shout.

Pilate was caught and he knew it. But he continued to look for a way out. His face changed again. "Longinus," he said, "if it is blood they want, it's blood that they will get. Take the prisoner and have him flogged with the scorpion. See to it!"

The leather strands of the scorpion whip incorporated sharp bronze, lead, glass, or bone pieces so that it would cause pain and destroy flesh.

Longinus knew what that meant. He, as well as all the soldiers in the cohort, knew the cruelty of the scorpion—a whip with braided thongs laced with either bronze, bone, lead, or bits of glass. Often, the whip was made of rawhide taken from a donkey because of its toughness and ability to hold the embedded bits of material without breaking. The punishment was so cruel that the Roman senate had passed a law forbidding its use to punish a Roman citizen, a woman, or any soldier—unless the soldier was a deserter. Because of its construction, the soldiers had a saying, "The hide of an ass, for the hide of an ass."

Flogging was often called the punishment "next to death" because the pain and damage the whip caused could bring someone to the very edge of death and make them wish for death. While the strands were only as long as an arm, they were brutal beyond belief. They were attached to a wooden handle that allowed a double-handed grip by the one wielding the whip.

The victim would be stripped of all clothing and either had his hands tied to a ring above his head, or had his arms wrapped around a standing column, or was draped over a fallen column. The one wielding the whip would bring it down on a diagonal with both hands. Not only would the whip lash the flesh, but then, when the sharp pieces in the strands had embedded themselves in the flesh, they were ripped away from the person, causing even more damage and pain. The person wielding the whip had to be sure the strands didn't wrap around to the front of the victim. If they did, they could eviscerate the victim and cause instant death. The aim was to cause pain, not death.

When the guard had worked the whip on one diagonal from the victim's neck to his calves, he would change the direction of the blows and cut across the victim's back from another angle, again working from neck to calves. The first blows would soften the skin and bruise the underlying muscle. The succeeding blows and ripping motion would begin to peel ribbons of flesh from the body, exposing bleeding muscle and quivering nerves.

Longinus had assigned one of the toughest and largest soldiers in the unit to wield the whip. As the soldier whipped Jesus, Longinus expected to hear curses, moans, and threats from the victim. But instead, Jesus turned and looked at his tormentor with a look of pity!

Who is this man? Longinus found himself asking again. He had never before encountered anyone with this endurance and strength.

When the flogging was finished, some of the other soldiers joined in the sport of mocking Jesus by taking the old royal robe used at Herod's palace and pressing it into Jesus' bleeding back and shoulders. One of the soldiers made a crown of thorns from the plants growing against the wall and then jammed it rudely down onto Jesus' head. Others hit him with sticks, driving the thorns deeply into his scalp and sending rivulets of blood down his face and neck. "Here he is—the king of the Jews!" they mocked. "Hail, king of the Jews!"

The correct greeting for the emperor was, "Hail Caesar!" accompanied by a military salute if you were a soldier. The soldiers were showing their utter disdain for the populace by mocking the prisoner. It was a way of saying, "If this is how we treat your king, just imagine what we will do to you!"

Then the soldiers scratched out a rough chess-type board in the dirt. When the "board" was finished, they threw dice to see what number would come up. The pips on the bone dice were dots with circles around them, representing the eyes of the gods. The soldiers would throw the dice and then howl with laughter as they would move Jesus to the position called for by that roll and number. Each position had a punishment attached to it. On one spot, they would hit him with a fist; on another, kick him; on another, yank his hair or beard, and so on. It was a way of saying, "Our gods can move you around like a chess piece. You are nothing more than a pawn! You can't control even your own movements. We, the Romans—and our gods—control you!" The treatment was the epitome of mockery.

Roman dice were made of bone, ivory, or bronze. The pips were meant to depict the eyes of the gods, who were thought to control the results of the roll.

Yet Jesus said nothing. Nothing at all. Longinus, watching the proceedings, was amazed at his endurance and calmness.

Who is this man? he kept asking himself.

When the soldiers had enough of their mockery, Pilate called for Jesus to be brought to the balcony. The contrast between Pilate—resplendent in his white toga—and Jesus—in his blood-spattered robe and crown of thorns—could have hardly been greater. One the conqueror; one the conquered. One with all power; the other a beaten prisoner. For a split second, Longinus wondered which was which.

Pilate pushed Jesus forward, saying, "Behold the man!"—as if to say, "Isn't this enough? I told you I find no fault in him; now here he is bloody and bruised. Isn't this what you wanted?"

The crowd roared, "Away with him! Crucify him! Crucify him!"

Longinus's proximity to Jesus allowed him to see that Jesus was still serene, though suffering greatly from the scourging and the various beatings and mockings he had endured. Jesus was as bloody as a battle sword but as unbroken as though made of the best metal forged in the refiner's fire.

Earlier in the ugly exchange with the crowd, the rabble had threatened, "If you don't deal with this man, you are no friend of Caesar!" Longinus knew that was a rank and calculated slap at Pilate. "Friend of Caesar" was a well-known term used of someone who had no reputation or position but who then, through nothing more than Caesar's whim, became a recipient of his gifts. The emperor semi-adopted the person, gave him food, clothing, and everything he needed to sustain life—but he was still a "nobody" in the eyes of his peers. He was just lucky enough to be given everything and was absolutely dependent on Caesar for everything.

Essentially, they were saying that Pilate was a "nobody"—that he was only important because his wife was from the royal family. Failure to deal with Jesus would mark Pilate as less than a "Friend of Caesar."

Longinus reached for his sword and was ready to order his soldiers into the crowd, to mow them down like the noxious weeds they were. *This rabble has insulted Pilate, and I won't stand for it!* his mind screamed.

Pilate, reading Longinus's posture and clenched hand on the gladius at his hip, held out his hand in restraint. He didn't want a bloodbath, and he didn't want this altercation to continue. He had been warned by Claudia, he had examined Jesus and pronounced him innocent, but he was caught in a trap. One man must die or there would be a riot and hundreds, if not thousands, would die, and his reputation would be damaged.

Questions for Thought and Discussion

1. Herod had a very bad reputation. Name three people you know who have strongly positive reputations. How valuable is a good reputation? Why? How can people build a good reputation? How strong is your reputation in general and as a Christian?

2. Herod "wanted to see Jesus." What are some positives of curiosity? Explain the difference between curiosity and commitment. How can you help people move from spiritual curiosity to deeper commitment?

3. Jesus changed Herod by ignoring him. What would it be like for you to know that God had turned away from you and was paying no attention to you? If you have felt that way, what were the circumstances? Read Psalm 62 in light of what happened to Herod and Jesus. Discuss and share your findings.

4. Claudia Procula's warning to Pilate was a clear instance of God using pagan beliefs to tell the truth. What does that tell you about God?

5. Make a list of the kinds of mockery Jesus endured. Recall a time when you were mocked. How did that feel, and what were the effects on you? How did you get beyond the mockery and put-downs? How can you build people up who have been mocked and shamed?

6. Roman dice were more than gaming pieces; they were the "eyes of the gods," directing decisions and fate. What would be similar practices and beliefs today? How can you help people look to Christ rather than to just "roll the dice" when it comes to decision-making? How do you make decisions? How do you consult Jesus as part of the process for your decision-making?

Chapter 19

THE CRUCIFIXION

The ranting crowd was threatening. Longinus was not at all pleased that Pilate had offered to surrender Barabbas. In fact, he thought that freeing that murderous monster was reprehensible. Barabbas was the man who had killed the young Roman soldier earlier in the week. When the troops had found Barabbas, they also found the unlucky soldier's *pugio* tucked into Barabbas's belt. It was proof enough for the Romans to condemn Barabbas to death. His crucifixion would be an ugly warning to others who might think of looking the wrong way at a Roman soldier or citizen. Rome was known as the "iron empire" precisely because the iron fist of Roman justice promised to crush all dissent. Pilate was weakening Rome's authority by offering to free Barabbas.

Longinus feared that Pilate was being manipulated into a position where he would have to give in to the temple authorities regarding Jesus. The whole incident had deteriorated into a power struggle between Caiaphas and Pilate; it also seemed to Longinus that it involved a deeper power struggle beyond his grasp.

Pilate's anger at the crowd was apparent. He had proclaimed three times that he found no fault in Jesus, yet he had him flogged and now he was preparing to hand him over for crucifixion. Longinus heard Pilate murmur to himself, "It's better to kill one man than a hundred."

Longinus understood Pilate's comment. Failure on his part to condemn Jesus was sure to spark a riot. The city was filled with pilgrims from all over the empire. If a riot broke out, the Romans would have to kill hundreds, if not thousands, to quell the disturbance. That kind of action would surely come to the attention of Tiberius—and just as surely cause trouble for Pilate. One man was simply not worth that much trouble. The procurator would save his own hide at the cost of this troublesome "king of the Jews." In combat, it isn't finesse that counts—it's survival. Pilate wasn't interested in finesse; he was focused on survival.

Before turning Jesus over to be crucified, Pilate called for the washbasin and towel he had used earlier that morning. Longinus wondered what Pilate was going to do with them. As soon as the towel and basin were delivered, Pilate began to wash his hands as a way of saying that he was innocent of this man's blood. More than that, Longinus knew enough of Jewish literature to recognize that Pilate was acting out one of the songs of David. The singer of Israel had written, "I will not sit with the ungodly, I will wash my hands in innocence." Pilate's action was his way of saying, "I am more righteous than you are. You wouldn't enter my courts for fear of defilement. Well, you are a bunch of phonies, and *I wouldn't be caught dead sitting down with the likes of you vile people.*"

The message wasn't lost on the crowd. They got it, loud and clear. They responded in kind: "His blood be on us!"

Pilate's next words were predictable: "Crucify him."

With those two words, Pilate sealed Jesus' fate. After uttering them, Pilate turned and went back to a weeping Claudia Procula.

Because Longinus was in charge of carrying out Pilate's orders, it fell his lot to be in charge of the crucifixion process. Of course, he had done it many times before. While crucifixion was always ugly, if it furthered the cause of Rome, he had few pangs of conscience about doing it.

This time, it was different, though—disturbingly different. The morning's events had brought him close to Jesus. Longinus had watched how he had handled himself with the crowds, with a king, and with Pilate. Even the beatings and flogging hadn't changed the man. Oh, they had changed his body to be sure, but none of the brutality had changed his spirit. That impressed Longinus.

The protocol for crucifixion called for flogging as part of the process. The fact that Jesus had already been flogged didn't matter. The crucifixion orders were standard and clear: "Prisoners condemned to die on the cross will be flogged first." That was that. There was no leniency because of a prior flogging. So, Jesus was flogged a second time. It nearly made Longinus sick.

The Crucifixion

Once the flogging was completed, each of the three men to die was forced to carry the crosspiece, or *patibulum,* to the place where they would die. The *patibulum* was eight to ten inches square, nearly seven feet long, and weighed as much as one hundred twenty-five pounds. It was placed behind the head of the condemned man, who had to balance it on his raw, bleeding shoulders. Then his outstretched arms were tied to the rough beam, ensuring that he wouldn't throw it down in an attempt to run away. The torture of death by crucifixion began long before the nails were driven into the bodies of the crucified.

As the two thieves stumbled along, they swore at the soldiers and the people who stood along the road to mock them. It was now about nine in the morning, and though it was spring, on this day the sun was already unmercifully hot. The prisoners were not allowed any liquid to drink. This was a deliberate plan to amplify their suffering.

Jesus was so weakened that he had trouble keeping up with the other two men. Several times, he stumbled and fell, the heavy crosspiece slamming him into the pebble-covered road. As he tried to stand, he would slide face first in the dirt. The crowd that followed from Pilate's judgment hall laughed and taunted, "He looks like a snake squirming on a hot rock!"

Longinus burned with indignation that these people would mock someone so wounded and yet so strong. But as distasteful as it was, he had a job to do, and he would do it.

Jesus stumbled and fell again and again. It was obvious that he wouldn't be able to carry the load to the hill of death—the place of the skull—just outside the walls of the city. Burning with anger, Longinus wheeled around to the crowd, drew his gladius, pointed it at the nearest man, and said, "You! You carry it for him!"

The man's eyes and mouth went wide with shock. He began to object, then thought better of it, gulped his fear down, and stepped over to Jesus. Two soldiers untied Jesus' arms from the *patibulum* and gave it to the man. Jesus struggled to his feet and helped him carry the load. Jesus seemed to be embracing his own death instrument!

Longinus gritted his teeth and grimly led the procession along, but he had the strange feeling that Jesus was somehow in charge, and that he—the Roman commander—was just an escort. At that thought, he shook his head as if to dislodge the idea. *That's insane,* he thought. *I am in charge. I'm always in charge. Rome is in charge. This man is just like any other pretender. He's nothing more than that. He will die because Rome has decreed it, and that's all there is to it. So ignore these doubts and get on with the job.* He remembered the hobnail pattern on his sandals—the man kneeling and begging for mercy. The message was still the same—no mercy from Rome.

Longinus led the procession to the top of Skull Hill, the place of crucifixion. The authorities had chosen this location because it was outside the city, so the city wouldn't be defiled, yet it was very visible, so the maximum number of people could see what went on and be warned to not even think of challenging Rome's rule. The location served as both a blot on the face of Jerusalem and an exclamation point to the power of Rome.

When Longinus reached the place where the upright posts for the crosses were laid out on the ground, he stopped. The crosspieces were untied from the two thieves and dumped on the ground. Four burly soldiers held the thieves, who by now were weak with exhaustion from packing their heavy loads up the hill. Their feet were raw and bleeding from the stony path on which they'd had to walk with bare feet. They were in no condition to escape, but the soldiers were taking no chances because the Roman custom, which later became written law, was that if any soldier allowed a prisoner he was guarding to escape, the soldier would pay the prisoner's penalty.

With Jesus, it was another matter. Longinus noticed that the man's initial terror had subsided as he walked along with Jesus, who talked to him as they carried the crosspiece together. Jesus had even changed *this* man!

Now the process of ending the condemned men's lives began a new phase. Everything up to this point was preparation for the pain to come from the crucifixion. The pain would be literally "excruciating." That word is derived from the Latin words *ex* and *cruces* and means "pain like that from the cross."

Once the crosspieces had been firmly attached to the uprights, the prisoners were stripped of all clothing—their last vestiges of human dignity—and slammed to the ground by the soldiers, who then wrestled them onto the rough-hewn beams. Two soldiers held each wrist, and two held the feet, while two more held the body of the victim firmly on the cross.

Then another soldier drew from a leather pouch a six-inch-long square spike that tapered from a large square head to a sharp point. He placed the nail between the bones of the wrist about an inch from the bend in the wrist. This spot was chosen because the median nerve ran there and the thick band of cartilage supporting the wrist would be just above the nail. This placement served two purposes: every time the body moved, the nail would tear at the median nerve, causing waves of fiery pain to burn through the arm and hand, and the cartilage band would support the weight of the body and keep the arm from ripping off the wood beam. The Romans considered anything between the elbow and fingertips to be the hand, so it could be said that the nails were driven through the hand. No nail driven through the palm of the hand would hold a person on the cross because the nail would rip through the tissues.

The hard edges of the square nails used in crucifixion tore raw nerves and tissue. The overlarge heads precluded escape.

The elbows and arms weren't fully stretched out, allowing the condemned man to twist his body slightly so he could pull himself up on the nails to catch a breath. Of course, each such movement would bring excruciating pain from the nails and from the rough wood against the raw, bleeding back.

The way the feet were attached to the upright beam varied. Often, the knees were bent slightly, one foot was held flat against the upright beam, and the other foot placed on top of the arch of the first foot. Then the soldier drove a single eight-inch spike through both arches, pinning them to the cross. This position caused all the body weight to rest on the nail, except when the condemned man pulled on the nails that pinned his hands to the crossbeam. Some crosses had a footrest so the feet could be more horizontal and they, rather than a nail, would bear the weight of the body. Sometimes, the ankles would be placed on either side of the beam and nailed there, but that positioning required two nails so it was not used as frequently. And sometimes the ankles were held together twisted sideways across the upright, one nail pinning both ankles. The twisted torso added greatly to the agony of the dying man—which was precisely the point.

A contingent of soldiers held Jesus while they waited for the two thieves to be nailed to their crosses. The two men howled with agony and yelled curses as their torment began.

Then Jesus was roughly thrust down onto the third cross. Longinus watched intently, thinking, *Now we'll see who he truly is.*

As the first nail penetrated his flesh, Jesus began to speak. What he said shocked all of the soldiers, including Longinus. Rather than shouting curses, Jesus began to pray, "Father, forgive them, they don't know what they're doing."

All of the soldiers were used to verbal abuse and cursing. This prayer for them as they were causing added pain to a man they had only an hour before mocked and flogged took them aback. The soldier with the hammer stopped in mid-swing, scarcely believing what he had heard. The soldiers looked to Longinus for direction. He merely nodded, and they finished nailing Jesus to the instrument of torture.

Once the nailing was completed, the crosses had to be raised upright and placed in the holes cut in the rocky hilltop to hold them. The three-foot-deep holes were just large enough for the upright to slide into and held the crosses upright for all to see.

Six soldiers were detailed to raise the crosses. Two held the base of the cross and two on each side looped ropes over the ends of the crosspieces just beyond the hands of the men pinned there. At a signal, the soldiers with the ropes began to pull the cross up as the two at the base began to lift it. When the cross was nearly upright, the two at the base centered the upright beam in the hole. The cross then slid three feet down into the socket and hit the solid bottom with a thud, causing the body on the cross to rip on the nails. New streams of cursing filled the air as the thieves' crosses collided with the immovable stone at the bottom of the hole.

Jesus' cross was positioned between the other two—a place reserved for the most notorious person being crucified on any given day. That marked him as the chief miscreant.

The crucifixion process was laden with other symbolism too. The fact that the crucified men were stark naked announced that they were nothing; they were exposed—men without honor. The embarrassment was meant to add to their shame. Their feet were four to five feet above the rocky ground—as if they had been rejected by the earth and were so vile they couldn't touch it again. Adding to the indignity, they were not high enough to be claimed by the gods either. They were caught in the middle of nothingness—a place of shame and agony and rejection by the gods and by humanity.

Because the shame was so overwhelming, families of those crucified were often too embarrassed to claim the bodies. So when the criminals died, their twisted, bloody bodies would be pried from their crosses and thrown into the city's burning dump.

When someone was crucified, a *titulus* was fixed to his cross announcing his name and crime. Pilate himself had dictated Jesus' *titulus*. It was written in Latin, Greek, and Aramaic—the three languages everyone in the region could read regardless of their origin. It said, "Jesus of Nazareth, king of the Jews."

When the temple leaders read the sign, they were furious. They saw it, as Pilate had intended them to, as saying bluntly, "Look at what we are doing to your king! If we treat your king this way, guess how we'll treat you!"

The leaders immediately sent a delegation to Pilate requesting that he change the wording on the *titulus* to say, "He said he was king of the Jews." That would completely change the message's meaning.

Pilate's response was abrupt. Essentially, he said, "In your face!" He felt manipulated by Caiaphas into crucifying Jesus. So now, in his bitterness, he would return insult for insult, hostility for hostility. He would have the last word for all to see. Caiaphas and his crew may have won the death of their antagonist, but Pilate would rub their faces publicly in the filth of their Pyrrhic victory. If they didn't like what he wrote, that pleased him to no end.

The priests and leaders stood at the foot of the cross, taunting Jesus with cries of "If God loves you so much, let Him come down and claim you!" "You say you are the son of God. Well, where is He?" Their mocking laughter was like salt in a raw wound.

The Centurion

One of the thieves joined them in their mockery, "If you are who you say you are, come down from the cross and save yourself—and us!" The other thief revealed that he had a different view. He said, "We deserve to die for what we have done, but this man hasn't done anything wrong!" Then, turning to Jesus, he pled, with tears streaming down his face, "Remember me when you come into your kingdom." It was a simple request—and a profound profession from the lips of a man whose life was being wrung from his tortured body.

Jesus' eyes brightened as he stood on the nail that had been driven through his feet and drew his body up the ragged, rugged wood by the nails in his hands to say, "I promise you today—you will be with me in Paradise." Then he slumped back down, scraping his raw back on the rough wood, the splinters tearing at what flesh was left and sending streams of fiery pain streaking through his body.

Longinus knew that when people were crucified, the intercostal muscles in the rib cage became cramped and paralyzed from the stress exerted by their position on the cross. That meant that for each breath, Jesus and the two thieves had to pull themselves up and then drop back down. The up-and-down motions amplified the pain caused by the nails, nerves, and rough wood.

Longinus then noticed that one of Jesus' followers was supporting a weeping, distraught woman who looked with love at Jesus. It was obvious that she must be his mother. Jesus nodded to them, pulled himself up on the nails, and began to speak. "Behold your son," he said, nodding to the woman. "Behold your mother," he said, nodding to the man. The exertion caused him to collapse as far down as the nails and stretched tissue would allow. As he slumped, his head banged against the cross, driving the crown of thorns deeper into his head.

Because Longinus was in charge of the crucifixions, he scanned the crowd continuously, looking for any signs of trouble. He was watching, lest anyone would be so foolhardy as to try to save the prisoners from their mandated deaths. As he looked around, he saw another weeping woman, whom he recognized as Mary of Magdala. Her reputation was well known among the cohort, and it wasn't spotless. But Mary had changed, softened, somehow been transformed. An inner glow—a kind of serenity—radiated from her in the midst of her sorrow.

Longinus found himself wondering yet again, *Who is this man—this Jesus? He changes everyone with whom he comes in contact: Marcus, Malchus, Herod,*

The Crucifixion

Pilate, Claudia, the man carrying the crosspiece, the thief, Mary. Where will it end? How will it end?

Just then, Longinus caught sight of Malchus standing beside Caiaphas the high priest. Malchus definitely had both ears—Longinus could see that. He could also see that Caiaphas's ridiculing of Jesus was troubling Malchus. He looked at Jesus and then glanced away with tear-glazed eyes and an agonized look on his face. He wasn't the same arrogant, pushy person who had come to claim Caiaphas's robes. He looked humbled, confused, and very uncomfortable.

Caiaphas, on the other hand, was oblivious to Malchus and to everyone else. His face was contorted with rage and hatred as he mocked Jesus and hurled insults at him. *His hostility seems demonic,* thought Longinus. *Hardly fitting for a man who is supposed to be a spiritual leader.*

Jesus pulled up on the nails again. Longinus knew he was about to speak, and he listened intently as Jesus' parched, blood-covered lips began to move. *"Eloi, Eloi, lama sabachthani?"* he cried out in utter agony, tears streaming down his face.

Longinus knew enough of the language to understand that Jesus had cried out, "My God, My God, why have You forsaken Me?" Apparently, the man was enduring some inner torture that exceeded the external pain of the crucifixion. He was feeling pain to the depths of his soul—something that profoundly puzzled Longinus, yet something that connected with him. He had felt some of that pulling pain at Gaius's death. He had wondered where the gods were then. The thought was unsettling—a pulling together of "then" and "now" in a whirl of distress.

Although it was now midday, the sky began to darken. Longinus looked up to see if a storm was gathering and discovered that there were no clouds. Yet the sun was darkening as though night was upon them. People looked around, wide-eyed. It wasn't an eclipse—it was lasting too long for that. It was as if even the sun refused to look down on the spectacle being played out on Skull Hill.

The soldiers became jumpy. The Romans believed that major omens from the gods involved the sky and heavenly bodies, so the darkening of the sun was a huge omen. Even Longinus felt his skin crawling under his armor. The darkness seemed to penetrate even the iron encasing his body, making him feel vulnerable—as naked and exposed as the criminals on the crosses.

"Men!" he shouted to his troops, "be especially vigilant. I don't know what is happening any more than you do, but we will remain in charge and at our stations. Understood?"

Yes, they understood. They would stand fast.

Not long after that, Jesus drew himself up on the nails again. He was going to speak again. Longinus knew the difference between the ragged movements that promoted breathing and those that portended speech.

His face twisted with the effort and the agony, Jesus rasped out, "I'm thirsty."

Of course he was thirsty. That was calculated to be part of the agony of crucifixion. Men who were crucified died from dehydration, exposure, and exhaustion. Physical exertion drained them of fluids; so now, along with waves of pain, came a raging thirst.

With a nod of his helmeted head, Longinus motioned to a soldier standing at the foot of Jesus' cross, among a group who had been dividing Jesus' clothing among them. The man poked a stick into a sponge and dipped the sponge in posca—a rotten vinegar wine used both to quench thirst and to act as an analgesic to diminish some of the pain. When he held it to Jesus' mouth, Jesus turned away, as if he wanted to feel every bit of the pain of the crucifixion.

The whole scene was becoming surrealistic to Longinus. What he expected to happen was not happening. What was unexpected was happening. Everything seemed upside down.

Longinus found himself riveted to every movement Jesus made. He was trying to figure out who this man was, what made him who he was, why he was so reviled by the temple authorities, how he could change so many people, and whether he was a king or an imposter.

Now Jesus was going to speak again. Would it be a curse on the Romans and the Jews? What would he say? He didn't have to wait very long to find out. Jesus pulled himself up on the cross and called out, "It is finished!" Then he slumped down again.

Finished? What was finished? The crucifixion was certainly not finished. Men could last several days before they died on a cross. It made no sense. The saying only added to the mysteries Longinus was trying to unravel about this man and the events swirling around him. He was drawn to the man's strength and courage and concern for others. He had even asked God to forgive the soldiers who were crucifying him! Longinus mentally replayed the events of the day. He thought of many things: the frantic look on Claudia Procula's face . . . her note about the gods warning Pilate to "leave this righteous man alone" . . . the words of Jesus from the cross . . . the crowds' raging that Jesus had claimed to be the son of God . . . the story of Malchus's miracle . . . Julius's telling about Jesus healing Pulcher . . . and finally, Gaius's death.

This final thought rattled Longinus deeply. He had told his dying son, "I will not leave you!" Yet, this Jesus had cried out, "My God, My God, why have You forsaken Me?" Longinus remembered Gaius's asking for a drink and his willingness to respond to his son. Longinus heard again Jesus saying, "I thirst," and saw the Roman response of rotten wine rather than cool water.

The swirling, confusing, troubling thoughts and memories caused Longinus's eyes and thoughts to leave Jesus momentarily. Suddenly, he heard Jesus cry out with a loud, resonant voice, "Father, into Your hands I commit My spirit!" It was not the cry of life ebbing out of a defeated man. It was more like a strong, trumpet-clear shout of victory.

Longinus's eyes darted to Jesus' face. What he saw startled him beyond anything he had experienced to this point. Jesus was as radiant as a conquering hero, his face and eyes bright with triumph, his words those of a victor delivering kingdoms to his ruler.

Then, as Longinus watched, transfixed by what was happening, it seemed to unfold in slow motion. Jesus' eyes flickered closed, his body relaxed against the nails, and his head dropped slowly down until his chin sank to his chest.

The moment Jesus' chin touched his chest, the earth began to tremble and buckle, and a flash of lightning lit up the dark city brighter than day. An ear-splitting crash of thunder followed the lightning. Then, in the eerie silence after the thunder had rolled away, when the very earth seemed to hold its breath, Longinus heard his own voice cry out, "This was God's Son!"

His words echoed and reverberated from the stone walls of Jerusalem like a trumpet blast. The troops under his charge stared at him with wide eyes and open mouths, but they knew better than to say a word. It seemed as if the world had stopped turning and everything hinged on what he had said.

Longinus had just committed high treason. The son of the gods was the emperor in Rome—not a dying man on a cross. Yet that burning flash of lightning, that resounding crash of thunder, the events of the day and of his entire life—all underlaid his clarion confession. He didn't understand where or how he came to cry out as he did, but it clearly came from the depths of his soul. The words were wrung out of what he had seen of this man—out of what he had heard. His cry had been an involuntary response from the recesses of his being.

Longinus had chosen to wear his trooper armor so he could identify with those he trained and led. If God were to speak to human beings, wouldn't He do the same thing? Wouldn't He identify with them, live among them, convey His message to them by example? That's what Jesus did.

Even by Roman standards, the omens pointed to Jesus! The sun going dark, the thunder and lightning, his being "lifted up" in the sky for all to see, Claudia Procula's warning of the omens in her dreams—it *all* supported Longinus's confession.

Instantly, however, Longinus's epiphany made him shake in ice-cold terror. Another conviction forced itself upon him: *I have been responsible for his death!* That thought nearly drove him to his knees.

Questions for Thought and Discussion

1. Pilate faced a dilemma. Where does the issue of ethics come into decision-making? It has been said that, "When facing a dilemma, one way to deal with it is to go above both sides for the answer." Do you agree, or disagree, and why?
2. Read Psalm 26:4–6 and then reflect on Pilate's response and his "washing his hands" of the judgment of Jesus. Was Pilate just ducking the issue, or was there more to his response? What spiritual decisions might you be trying to duck right now?
3. How would you have felt if you had been asked to carry a cross as Simon of Cyrene was? When have you been drafted to do something you didn't elect to do? What was it like, and what was the end result?
4. Jesus faced physical, social, religious, mental, spiritual, and other agonies on the cross. Which do you think was the worst? Why did you pick that one?

5. When was the last time you prayed for someone who was deliberately trying to hurt you or cause you trouble? Will you do that now, before you go on? "Father, forgive them . . ."

6. When and how did you come to the conclusion and confession that Jesus is the Son of God? What events and processes brought you to that point? If you are not yet there, what holds you back?

Chapter 20

MEANING, MERCY, AND GUARD DUTY

The thought that he had participated in the death of the one he had called the Son of God weighed heavily on Longinus. His mind raced to find meaning in the muddle and mix of what had gone on that day. Had he made a mistake?

In Roman society, if soldiers made a mistake in battle resulting in their *aquila*—the golden eagle standard of the legion—being captured, the penalty was to *decimate* the unit. That meant every tenth man would be beaten to death by his friends and fellow soldiers as a way of atoning for the sin of losing the standard. The contrast with what Longinus saw in Jesus was remarkable. He took the blow. He paid the price so others could go free, even to the point of praying and asking forgiveness for those who crucified him.

And Longinus had played a part in his death.

There was no time to deliberate, though. Longinus must report Jesus' death to Pilate, as he had been told to do. Pilate had more than a passing interest in the outcome. Perhaps Claudia Procula's message prompted that, or the fact that he had thrice said he found no fault in Jesus. At any rate, Pilate needed to know how and when Jesus died.

Pilate had seen the sun darken, had felt the earthquake, heard the thunder, and seen the lightning too. Now, as he considered all the omens and Longinus's report of what he had seen, he went pale. He was shaken.

"He died that soon?" he asked. "He should have lasted longer—maybe several days. You're sure he is dead?"

Longinus verified his report, adding that the thieves were still alive.

"Go back and see that the thieves die too," commanded Pilate. "The temple authorities want them dead and down before sunset. They told me the bodies cannot remain there over the High Passover Sabbath day. Having them there would be a serious transgression of their laws and their sensibilities. Speed up their deaths so they can be removed before sunset. I want no more trouble with them."

There was a sure way to speed up the deaths. It was a practice called *crucifracture*. An iron bar was used to break the bones in the lower legs of those on the crosses. Once the bones were broken, creating compound fractures, the excruciating pain would prevent the crucified person from using his legs to raise himself so he could breathe. He would pass out and then suffocate.

The screams of the thieves as their legs were broken sent shivers up Longinus's spine. When the soldiers came to Jesus, they hesitated. Longinus's exclamation about this man being the Son of God was still clear in their minds. It was obvious that he was dead, but they had to be sure. There could be no mistakes about the finality of a Roman execution order, or the soldiers and their commander would be executed.

Seeing their hesitation, Longinus ordered them not to break Jesus' legs. He felt that Jesus had suffered enough indignity with multiple beatings, mockery, and nails. "No!" he commanded, "Give me a spear. I'll see to it." In his mind, Jesus, the Warrior, deserved some respect even though he was dead. In an act of mercy, Longinus thrust the spear upward into the heart of Jesus. When he did, blood flowed freely down the spear onto his hands. Now he literally had on his hands the blood of the one he had proclaimed to be God's Son.

The thieves died quickly. The nails were pulled, and their bodies were to be taken to the city dump to be burned. As the thieves were being removed from their crosses, two wealthy and influential men informed Longinus that they had appealed to Pilate and he had given them permission to remove and bury Jesus' body.

Longinus felt a wave of relief that Jesus wouldn't be sent to the dump. He didn't know what he would have done if Joseph of Aramathea and Nicodemus hadn't come for the body. But they had come, and he was glad of that. At least, Jesus would have a decent burial, even if he suffered an indecent death. Any warrior deserved that as a minimum.

The Centurion

Pilate had told Longinus to turn things over to the *optio* after the crucifixion detail had finished their work. Longinus was more than glad to go off duty and to be with Julia. He had much to share with her—and with Julius and Livia too. So, he headed to Julius's home after the crosses had been taken down and the bodies removed. It had been a long day. An ugly day. An unforgettable day.

As Longinus approached Julius's quarters, he could hear the gravel crunch under the hobnails of his sandals. They bore the design he had thought of more than twenty years earlier—the man kneeling, begging for mercy. And true to the messages on the sandals, Rome had shown no mercy to Jesus. He, however, had shown mercy to the thief, to his mother, and to the very ones who had nailed him to the cross. The eyes of Jesus and Longinus had met, and when they did, Jesus' eyes spoke a language more potent than Rome's military might. That was part of what had prompted Longinus's declaration at the cross.

"Longinus! I am so glad to see you," he heard Julia's sweet voice say as he entered the house. "Come, I have water so you can bathe and scented oil for where your armor has chafed your skin."

"You're far too good to me," Longinus said, and he smiled at Julia. "Yes, this has been a very long day."

"The darkness, earthquake, lightning, and thunder all told us something momentous was happening, but we didn't know what it was. Then Marcellus Sylvanus told us after he had reported to Pilate."

"Marcellus told everyone?"

"Yes. He was like an artesian spring. He just poured out everything that he had seen and heard."

"Then . . . what I said . . ."

"We know what you said, Longinus," responded Julia. "And we believe you were right."

"You—'we'—believe I was right? 'We' who?"

"I believe you were right. So do Julius and Livia. We believe that Jesus was—is—God's Son."

Longinus was stunned. He just stood there, mouth agape, eyes wide open in surprise.

"Go, take off the armor and bathe," Julia said, smiling sweetly. "We can talk more after you have relaxed a bit. Julius and Livia have prepared a meal for us."

As Longinus sponged off the sweat and grime of the day, he kept thinking how refreshing the cool water felt on his skin. He'd felt like a rooster in an oven today under the hot sun. He wondered if it were possible to bake in your own armor. Sweat had poured from his body, and he was glad to have had his canteen available. Then, out of thin air or the recesses of his memory, came a rasping voice—*"I thirst."*

As if a bolt of lightning had struck nearby, Longinus flinched, his emotions raw and vibrating. *I had water; he had nothing. I had armor; he was exposed. I had power; he was powerless. I showed no mercy; he was merciful to all.*

Longinus, Julia, Livia, and Julius lingered long after their evening meal and discussed the events of the day, the man, and the meaning of it all. "You know," observed Julius, "I saw Jesus many times when I was posted in Capernaum. I heard him teach, and believe me, no one ever taught as he did. He even showed kindness to us Romans. That's why, when Pulcher fell so ill, I went to him for help."

"And he healed Pulcher," Longinus said.

"Yes, he did," responded Julius. "That's when Livia and I began to believe he was more than a man. However, it wasn't just because of Pulcher's healing, but also because of the way he treated everyone. That's why we shared what we did with Julia about our belief, and why she suggested that you call Jesus to heal Gaius."

"You must all hate me for what I've done," whispered Longinus, barely able to form the words.

"No, Longinus," responded Julius. "I heard him say he would die. He said that was his destiny. You were merely a part of that destiny. But there is more."

"More? What more can there be? I helped execute the man!"

Julius took a deep breath and continued, "I heard him say that when he died, he would come back to life again after three days."

"You mean like the Mithra account?" Longinus asked.

"No, not like that at all," Julius responded. "He said his death and return to life would fulfill the words of the Hebrew prophets—that he would bring peace and forgiveness to those who believe in him. That he would bring eternal life to those who believe in him."

"You don't understand. I killed him!" moaned Longinus. "I crucified him and then rammed a spear into his side. His blood is on my hands—on my soul!"

"No, Longinus, you didn't kill him," responded Julia in a steady, strong voice. "You didn't kill him."

"I was in charge! My spear went into his side . . . into his heart."

"True," said Julius. "But Julia is right. Look at it again. He was dead before you used your spear, right?"

That was true.

"Look, my friend," Julius continued. "We Romans didn't kill him. We beat him, we mocked him, we put the nails in his flesh, but we did not kill him. *You* did not kill him. What were his last words?"

"He spoke only seven times from the cross," recalled Longinus. "Each saying was short—terse."

"Yes," said Julia. "But what were his *last words?*"

"Father, into Your hands I commit—"

Suddenly, it was as if someone had lit a hundred torches. Longinus stopped in midsentence. "That's right! *He gave his life to his Father!*"

"Then what happened?" urged Livia.

"After he said that, his head dropped . . . and . . . he . . ." Longinus's voice trailed off for a moment. Then he continued, "He died."

"That's right," said Julius. "He *gave up his life.* You didn't take it. You didn't kill him. He chose to die. He willed to die. It was part of his destiny."

"Yes!" responded Longinus. "And I thrust the spear into his side because I wanted to spare him any more mutilation. I wouldn't let them break his legs. I tried to show him—"

"Mercy," whispered Julia.

"Yes . . . mercy. I wanted to show him mercy," sighed Longinus.

"He will show you mercy, too," Julius said.

Longinus struggled to understand what these people whom he trusted most in the whole world were saying to him. "I don't understand it," he said. "It doesn't fit anything I know."

"Yes, it does, my husband. You've told me a hundred times what your first mentor taught you: 'Listen to your inner voice. Go with your heart.' So now, listen to that inner voice. Go with your heart," said Julia.

They talked until the oil lamps began to burn out and sent smoky curls ascending into the night.

"I need to get some rest," Julius announced. "Tomorrow is the High Holy Day—Passover. It is supposed to be a day of 'Sabbath rest,' but I fear great unrest will be the reality."

In the privacy of their guest quarters, as Julia was applying oil to Longinus's aching muscles, his thoughts returned to Jesus. He had hurt too, but no one had eased his pain. Longinus had friends, yet Jesus cried out that he had been forsaken. Around and around the thoughts churned as Longinus remembered the events of the day.

Longinus slept fitfully that night, if it could be called sleep at all. He kept hearing *"Father, forgive them."* . . . *"You will be with Me in Paradise."* . . . *"Father, forgive them."* . . . *"I thirst."* . . . *"Father, forgive . . ."*

Dawn came painfully early. No matter. Longinus had long been awake, watching as the sky went from blue-black and star-studded to the brilliant redorange of sunrise.

Red—like blood. Even the sky reminded Longinus of the day before. Would nothing ever be the same again?

Everything seemed to remind him of Jesus. Julia's peaceful sleep and the look of contentment on her face reminded him of Jesus. In spite of the torture he had experienced, Jesus had a look of profound peace on his face even in death.

Only one thing could be done: he must get up and go on duty. That's why Pilate had brought Longinus with him—duty. Maybe the military routine would bring some order to his fractured thinking. He hoped so.

When he got to the guard room, the soldiers were talking about the justafter-dawn visit of yet another delegation from the temple. They had come into the tower and asked to meet with Pilate in his audience hall—something they had refused to do just the day before because it would make them unclean for the High Sabbath of Passover. Yet they had come with no hesitation into the chambers on the holy day itself!

Longinus was puzzled by the behavior, so he asked the soldiers, "What did they want of us this time?"

"We don't know, sir," they replied. "Pilate saw the delegation, and they left just before you came in."

Just then, one of Pilate's pages ran into the room. "Oh, Longinus, am I ever glad to see you!" he said, "Pilate sent me to ask you to report to him immediately. He wants to see you right away. It seems very important, but I don't know what it's all about."

Pilate was gazing out a window, elbow on the armrest of his chair and his fist supporting his chin. He seemed absorbed in thought. At the sound of Longinus's sandals, he looked around and was pleased to see him.

"The priests and other leaders of the Jews have suggested that we post a guard at the tomb of Jesus," he said. "It seems there is a rumor racing around that the man said he would come back to life three days after his death. They want to make sure no one steals the body and perpetrates the myth of his resurrection. I want you to assign a century of soldiers to guard that tomb. It seems a prudent thing to do."

Longinus recalled that Julius had said he had heard Jesus speak of his coming back to life three days after his death. Longinus spoke immediately, and his words surprised himself nearly as much as they did Pilate. "Sir, with your permission, I volunteer to be in charge of that detail personally."

"You don't need to do it, Longinus," responded Pilate. "Send Marcus or one of the other centurions. It isn't worth your time. You've had enough trouble because of that man Jesus—and so have I. Send someone else."

"Sir, in a way, I do need to do it. I want to see for myself—"

"I understand, Longinus," Pilate interrupted with a smile. "I trust you and your honesty. I'd rather have you there than anyone else. That man has caused too many problems already. We certainly don't need more. Permission is gratefully granted."

"Consider it done, sir," Longinus responded.

"Make it absolutely official. Seal the tomb with the signet ring I gave you. No one would be fool enough to breach Rome's official seal," concluded Pilate.

"Consider it done, sir," responded Longinus again, this time with a smart salute.

"Good!" said the procurator. "Maybe we'll be able to put an end to this thing once and for all."

Questions for Thought and Discussion

1. The temple leaders had scruples against going into a Roman building because of the Passover, yet they came into a Roman fortress with no seeming trouble when they wanted a guard posted at the tomb. Why and when do people bend rules? Have you ever bent any rules? Which ones, and why?

2. Longinus's sandals proclaimed that the Romans walked *on* mercy. Jesus walked *in* mercy. Contrast those two points of view on how to live. Which one is closest to your walk? How will others see that?

3. After Longinus had confessed Jesus to be the Son of God, he began to waver and have doubts. What has caused you to doubt your initial confession and commitment to Christ? Who or what brought you back to that original confession and commitment?

4. Discuss the concept of the Roman soldier's spear in Jesus' side being an act of mercy. How do you show mercy to others?

5. Why do you think Longinus volunteered to lead the guard contingent at the tomb when he could have delegated that duty to someone else? What would you have likely done in the same circumstances? Why?

6. Compare and contrast the concepts of decimation and punishment with the grace of God through Christ. How can you use that information to reach out to others with healing rather than pain?

Chapter 21

WATCHING AND WAITING

When Longinus told Julia that he had volunteered for the tomb watch, she smiled, cocked her head, raised an eyebrow, and said, "That doesn't surprise me at all, husband. I would have been surprised if you hadn't volunteered."

He responded lightly, "I thought you might be a little upset that I chose to be with a dead man rather than my lovely, lively wife."

"I know you too well, Longinus. You have to see how it all comes out, don't you?"

"Yes, I do. The man was—is—the most compelling person I have ever encountered—other than you, of course," he said.

"And Pilate?" she asked.

"Pilate is more than willing for me to be in charge of the detail. In fact, Julia, he wants me to seal the tomb with the signet ring he gave me years ago." As he spoke, he held up the bronze ring with the stylized imperial eagle carved into it. He had worn that ring longer than he had his wedding ring. In many ways, he was wed to the legions as much as to Julia. Fortunately, she understood that his commitment to the military didn't diminish his commitment to her.

"I'll assemble the century of troops this morning. We'll be on duty from this evening until we are relieved midmorning tomorrow," he said. "I'll make a full report to Pilate. He said we can begin our leave time after that. Marcus will take over for the balance of the time Pilate remains in Jerusalem and see to it that he is escorted safely back to Caesarea. So, Julia, my dearest, we'll soon have some time together when we can start a new phase of our life."

Julia gathered some dates, nuts, bread, and fruit for Longinus to take with him, wrapping them in a colorful cloth. Smiling and handing the food to him, she said, "You may be guarding a dead man, but I don't want you to starve to death doing it. Now, go."

Signet rings were used to seal items of importance. The eagle was a common insignia of Rome and the Roman military.

When Longinus began to make up the century that would guard the tomb later that day, some soldiers volunteered for the detail—soldiers who had been at Skull Hill when Jesus died. They had seen what Longinus had seen and had heard what Jesus said. Like Longinus, they too wanted to see what the outcome would be. Longinus wasn't the only one whom Jesus had affected.

One of the younger volunteers who had served on the crucifixion detail had also been on the detail Marcus led to arrest Jesus in the garden and so had witnessed the incident with Malchus's ear. He came to Longinus privately. "Sir, what you said out there . . . on the hill . . . about his being a son of the gods . . ."

"Actually, I called him *the* Son of God."

"Yes, sir, *the* Son of God. Ah, well," he stammered, "how did you come to that conclusion, sir?"

Without giving Longinus a chance to respond, the young man continued, "As for me, I saw him heal a severed ear. I saw him comfort people while we were killing him. He prayed for us while we were nailing him to the cross. I mean . . . he had such a peace about him. I want that kind of peace too, sir."

"I understand, soldier," said Longinus, placing his hand on the young trooper's shoulder. "Believe me, I have seen too many battles, too much war and brutality. Peace would be a very welcome thing. So we will see whether he brings peace—or whether it's just an illusion. Right now, we have work to do, and I need your help. Grab that leather bag on the table and come with me."

The soldier obeyed, scooping up the smooth leather bag. As he did so, he realized that it contained several sticks of sealing wax and a roll of stout flax cord. His quizzical expression brought a smile to the centurion's face.

"It's to put the official seal of Rome on the tomb," Longinus said. "Once we tie the cords across the entrance to the tomb and then seal it, there'll be no way anyone can tamper with the burial without breaking the seal—an official seal placed on behalf of the emperor," Longinus said in answer to the unspoken question. "Do you know what the penalty is for the unauthorized breaking of an official Roman seal?"

"Yes, sir!" responded the soldier proudly. "That is an offense punishable by immediate death. On the spot. No exceptions. No mercy."

"You have learned well, soldier. We'll seal the tomb with this ring. It has an image of an eagle engraved on it—the same eagle as is on our helmets. Pilate gave me this ring when I was about your age, shortly after I joined the legions."

"You've known Pilate that long?" questioned the young trooper.

"Yes, and it's quite a story. If things get boring tonight, I may tell you about it. But now, let's go set the seal of Rome on the tomb and fulfill Pilate's orders."

As Longinus led the contingent of soldiers through the winding streets of Jerusalem, they made no attempt to be quiet. In fact, just the opposite. Roman soldiers routinely made plenty of noise as they marched. Their hobnailed sandals grated loudly on the paving stones, their armor and leathers and weapons clanged and banged and made quite a cacophony. The intent was to tell people that Rome was on the march and they'd better get out of the way. The message was that the soldiers could breach the door of any household as easily as the sound of their march penetrated into their homes. Longinus led the contingent, his red robe flowing behind him. The troops counted cadence as they marched behind with their commander.

By the time they got to the tomb, the few guards who had been temporarily placed there were gathering their belongings in anticipation of being relieved from their rather boring duty. They hadn't thought that guarding a dead man was worth the time and effort, but the decision wasn't theirs—just the orders.

The day was beginning to close, and the waning rays of the sun were striking the white marble walls of the temple and bathing them in golden light. The peace represented by the temple stood in high contrast to the coercion represented by the soldiers with their weapons and blood-red shields. The vivid difference jolted Longinus into reflecting on the contrasts surrounding the man whose tomb he was there to guard.

He vividly recalled the angry, vitriolic accusations the hate-filled mob had yelled out in contrast with the words of the crucified Jesus: *"Father, forgive"* . . . *"You will be with Me in Paradise."* . . . *"Father, into Your hands . . ."* Then there were the telling words of the young soldier who had been drafted to help seal the tomb: *"Sir, I want that kind of peace in my life."*

Peace, thought Longinus. *It is a good and lofty ambition, but how do you get there? There is the* Pax Romana, *but that has been won with the sword. How does one find inner peace?*

His reverie ended abruptly, as the contingent left the gate of Jerusalem and entered the burial area outside the city. Some of the tombs were natural limestone caves that had been converted into burial chambers for common folks. Some tombs were carved laboriously from living rock to hold the bodies of the wealthy and well-recognized. Wealthy men had forced the stone to yield sanctuaries of serenity deep within the cool rock. Such was the tomb they were called to guard.

Longinus recognized the tomb, for he had been there when Jesus' body was put there late Friday afternoon. He had watched as the battered body turned ashen gray, matching the cold stone. He had observed as the women bathed the body and then wrapped it in linen cloth. He had seen again the gaping wound made by the spear he had thrust into Jesus' side. He had stood back and watched

Joseph and Nicodemus as they laid Jesus' body in the vault.

Now, here he was again. This time, he wasn't present as an observer but to put Rome's guarantee of finality on the place by sealing the tomb with his ring.

As the group came to a halt, Longinus surprised them with a terse order, "Roll the stone away from the entrance. I will inspect the inside before we seal it forever."

Well, that did make sense. It would be important to know for sure that the body was still there before they sealed the entrance.

It took six strong soldiers to roll back the stone that blocked the entrance to the tomb. Even though it had been designed to provide access to the vault, it was no easy task to gain that access. When the grunting, groaning soldiers had rolled the stone back, Longinus took a torch and stepped into the tomb. The body of Jesus was right where he had seen Nicodemus and Joseph place it earlier.

A quick look convinced him also that it was the same body. He recognized the intricate pattern in which the grave cloth had been wound around it. More than that, he noticed the spot on the side that marked where his spear had entered the body. Some fluids had drained and stained the winding cloth. There was no mistake. This was the body of Jesus. Convinced, he exited the tomb and had the soldiers roll the stone back into place. Then Longinus signaled the young trooper with the sealing materials to come and assist him with the work at hand while there was still some daylight left.

The young soldier pulled out a small bronze lamp, lit the wick, and began to melt the red sealing wax as Longinus tied several knots in the flax cord. When there was a ball of softened wax, Longinus pressed it against the stone wall of the tomb to the upper left of the stone that covered the entrance. When the wax had begun to harden, he pressed a knot on one end of a cord into the wax and then took his ring off and used it to impress the eagle emblem into the wax, forcing it deeply into the material to secure everything tightly.

Next, he took another ball of softened wax, pressed it into place on the stone wall of the tomb to the lower right of the rolling stone door, took the loose end of the cord that had been embedded in the wax on the upper left of the door, pulled it snugly across the door, embedded it in the wax on the lower right, and sealed it with his ring. There was now a taut flax cord firmly in place diagonally across the entrance stone and anchored on the wall of the sepulcher. Then he repeated the process, this time starting at the upper right and going to the lower left. Thus an "X" of cords, embedded in wax and sealed there, secured the entrance stone.

One more thing was needed. Longinus had the soldier melt a large glob of wax and place it on the rolling stone where the cords crossed. He pressed the cords deeply into the wax, stuck another layer of wax on top of the "X," and used his signet ring to mark that junction as well.

Examining his work, Longinus was satisfied that no one could move the stone from the entrance in any direction without breaking several seals—and thereby making it obvious that the tomb had been violated (and ensuring their own death should they be caught). The tomb was secured.

Then it struck him: the red sealing wax looked like the drops of blood that had fallen from his hand after he had thrust the spear into Jesus. They looked like the crimson stains left on the cold, hard stone of Golgotha. He noticed one more striking thing: the placement of the seals—five of them—coincided with the pips on his ring, the one Julia had given to him with the prayer that the gods would watch over him north, south, east, west, and where he was now. It was the same as the markings for the number five on the dice used to mock the man now sealed behind stone. He just stood there, looking at the red spots. Remembering. Wondering.

Longinus recalled that Julius had told him Jesus said he would come to life after three days. He remembered the words of Pilate, repeating what the temple authorities had said about three days. As the Jews calculated time, yesterday, Friday, was day one because Jesus had died before sunset. That day, the Sabbath, was the second day. So the third day would begin at sundown, which was occurring right about then. That's why the temple leaders had requested a large guard for that evening and on through the next day.

What would happen? Longinus was there to find out. Julius, Livia, and even Julia said they believed what he said was true—that this man was more than a man, that he was the Son of God. Time would tell. He would know within twenty-four hours. Something deep inside him had to know. *"Follow your heart . . ."*

The Centurion

As the sun set and darkness began to snatch light from the sky, the soldiers heard the shofar horn sounding from the temple walls, marking both the end of the Passover Sabbath and the beginning of a new day and a new week.

Longinus's thoughts turned to Julia. He looked forward to having time off with her—a much-needed break and a new beginning for both of them. There were major decisions to make. He had put in enough time with the legions to retire, but he also had seniority enough to continue on to greater assignments and responsibilities. Julia and he had avoided discussing Gaius's death. They needed to do that now too. Yes, the next few weeks would bring a turning point in their lives—that he knew for sure.

The soldiers passed the hours of darkness talking about the quality of the legion's food, the best and worst assignments they'd had, where they wanted to go next, where they wanted to retire, and the latest rumors rampant in the barracks. Longinus had to smile when the soldiers complained about their food. He remembered with some pangs of pain the near-deadly meals he and the other seven soldiers in his group had cooked in their earlier days in the legions. Julia's culinary skills were among the many blessings marriage had brought to him. She was prize enough—and he loved her deeply—but the fact that she was an excellent cook was a welcome added benefit.

Several of the more senior soldiers in the century began to select groups to rotate as pickets posted away from the main body of troops and to organize the rest into segments who would remain awake and alert while the rest slept. When the plans had been formed, the senior soldier in each group reported to Longinus. "Sir, the schedule has been set. Here is a listing of who will be in command of each segment through the night. If you approve of the plan, we will execute it immediately."

Longinus reviewed and approved the plans, saluted the soldiers, and asked them to implement the plans laid to guard the tomb against anyone who might attempt to steal, or otherwise tamper with the body of Jesus and the will of Rome.

Longinus hadn't had to tell his soldiers what to do. His training had taught them what had to be done, and they took initiative to get it done. His training was effective, and they responded like the professionals he had taught them to become.

As commander, Longinus had been given the roster notes on a double-sectioned wax tablet known as a *tabula*. The design of the piece made it practical in many ways. When folded, it was small enough to be carried easily and the soot-blackened beeswax "pages" were protected from damage by the wooden covers. The wax could be cleared by exposing it to sunlight or to a burning firebrand, either of which would melt the wax, thus erasing the contents and providing a *tabula rasa,* or "blank slate," on which new messages could be written with a bronze stylus.

"Sir, you may rest as you please. If there is any disturbance, we will wake you," informed one of the senior soldiers in charge of the rotational schedules.

"Thank you. I shall do that. If there is any disturbance or any hint of one, let me know immediately," Longinus replied. He trusted his troops with his very life, and they trusted him with theirs. There was a strong sense that they all belonged to a team. And mutual respect and total professionalism marked who they each were.

Shortly after that, about the midwatch in the night, Longinus laid out his bedroll and drifted off to a restless sleep that was interrupted by a dream of the crucifixion and the crucified Jesus who lay in the tomb only yards away. One part of his dream was particularly disturbing: he was trying to wash the blood from his hands and spear, but the more he washed, the worse it got, until the water in the basin was crimson.

Then, as he lay dreaming, the ground began to shake, and Longinus woke up. *Was the ground actually shaking, or was it part of my dream?* he wondered. But in an instant, he knew he hadn't dreamed it. The ground buckled and heaved again as if it were an ocean. Its violence had him grasping at a nearby rock for support. By the light of the nearly full moon, he surveyed the area, and what he saw was frightening: his soldiers were stumbling around and falling as if they were drunk as the earth beneath their feet rolled. The terror in their eyes was unmistakable.

Suddenly, their terror tripled as the sky lit up with brilliant white light. It wasn't lightning; it was actually brighter than a bolt of that white-hot brilliance. When they shielded their eyes, they saw a being clothed in blinding brilliance descending from the sky directly to the entrance of the tomb. The soldiers who were closest to the majestic being stumbled away from it in terror. The being stepped to the stone blocking the entrance to the tomb and with one sweep of his hand rolled it away as if it were a pebble.

Longinus's heart was beating so wildly, he thought it might burst or jump out of his chest. He wanted to move, but he seemed rooted to the still-heaving ground. He had never experienced such absolute fear.

The bright being called into the tomb, "Son of God! Come out! Your Father calls You!"

At that summons, Longinus felt as if he had been slammed by a warhorse at full gallop. The being had used the same words he had used: *Son of God.*

In the silence that followed, every eye was riveted on the hole in the rock that was the tomb entrance and from which blinding light now radiated as if the tomb contained a thousand suns. Then Longinus saw him—the man he had pierced. The man he had called the Son of God. He saw Jesus walking out of the tomb, alive!

Longinus knew Jesus was dead when they took him down from the cross. He had verified that with a thrust of his spear. He knew death when he saw it and when he had caused it—as he had many times in battle. Instinctively, and without thought, he drew his gladius.

As Jesus strode majestically out of the tomb, his eyes again locked onto the eyes of the centurion. Longinus knew that Jesus had the right and the power to take his life. Instantly, he became aware of the *gladius* he held in a white-knuckled grip. Then a curious thought flashed through his mind: *How do you kill a man who has come back from the dead and is the Son of God who holds all power?*

At that thought, he tasted the metallic flavor of fear and collapsed to the ground. And, much as had happened when the barbarian had dealt him a nearly fatal blow early in his career, everything went black.

Questions for Thought and Discussion

1. Longinus had numerous commitments—to Julia, to Pilate, to his friends, to his soldiers, and to himself. Make a list of your commitments. Cut the list up and rearrange it to reflect the most important commitments you have. Where is God and your relationship with Him on the list?

2. One of Longinus's young troopers expressed his need for inner peace. How do you think people obtain that kind of peace? Explain.

3. Romans used a signet ring to seal things. What would be a modern equivalent of the Roman seal? What are the functions of a seal? Look up some biblical references to "seal," and share what you find.

4. The soldiers attempted to make the tomb secure. How and when have you thought you could make things secure on your own, only to find that to be far from reality? What did you learn from that experience?

5. Consider the *tabula* mentioned in this chapter—the instrument used to record events, lists, names, and details. Reflect on how to clear the *tabula* in your life and have a fresh, clean start. Consider: the Son and the Holy Spirit can offer the warmth to clear it so the past is forever gone. What do you want the Son and the Spirit to clear up and clear out for you?

6. Compare the omens occurring at Jesus' death with the omens at His resurrection. What might that say to a Roman hearing the story for the first time? What does it mean to you?

Chapter 22

NEW BEGINNINGS

When Longinus's eyes began to focus and he could breathe again, he staggered to his feet. His *gladius* lay in the dust, where it had fallen from his hand. He picked it up, wiped it clean, and put it back into the scabbard.

Looking around him, he saw soldiers lying on the ground, as though slaughtered in battle, and others stumbling around as though blind. Still others sat on the ground, dazed and wide-eyed.

"What . . . ?" "Did you see . . . ?" "Who . . . ?" the questions tumbled from the soldiers.

"Check the tomb," Longinus called hoarsely to the soldiers nearest its door. They stared at him as though he had asked them to march into a fire-belching volcano. It wasn't insubordination but abject terror that rooted them in place.

Longinus struggled to his feet and staggered toward the open tomb, grabbing a burning torch as he went. He felt his body shake with fear. Taking a deep breath, he stepped in. Light from the flickering torch he carried caused shadows to dance on the walls, but Longinus's eyes were riveted to the stone bench where the body of Jesus had been placed—to the spot where he had seen it only hours before. Now the space was empty—except for the grave clothes in which Jesus had been wrapped. They had been carefully folded and placed on the bench.

Longinus's mind was racing, searching for meaning. He recalled a Jewish table custom: when someone got up to refill his dish at a meal, to inform the servants not to clear his place, the custom was for that person to fold his napkin neatly and leave it at his place. The message was, "I'll be back." If, however, the person had finished eating, he would wad the napkin up and place it on the table. That meant, "I have finished." Jesus had folded the linens. He was back!

Longinus also recalled vividly when he had to decide to pick up his newborn son, who lay naked and exposed. Now he had experienced God the Father picking up His Son from within the ground and lifting Him up in life. The Son had been naked, exposed, vulnerable, and rejected. Now He had been accepted by the Father, who had unmistakably declared the lineage and value of His Son.

Then Longinus thought, *I must inform Pilate immediately! Jesus might be headed there to even the score with him.* Longinus bolted from the open tomb like an arrow from a bow, and he shouted to his soldiers, "Form up in ranks and move to the Antonia Tower—on the double!"

Turning to the next-most-senior soldiers, he gave them orders: "Move the troops back in formation. I'll go directly to Pilate's palace and report to him." And with that, he was off and down the path at his fastest walking pace. He didn't run because if he had, he would surely have attracted attention, and he did not want attention.

On the way into the city, he met an ashen-faced delegation from the temple. Apparently, the earthquake had rattled them too, and now they were running to the tomb to see what had happened. When they saw him headed toward the city and away from the tomb, they assumed—correctly—what it meant.

"What happened?" they inquired of Longinus, as they turned to walk with him.

"I don't report to you," snapped Longinus. "If you want to know, come hear it as I tell Pilate."

"No need to do that," responded one of the group. "Here's a bag of coins for you and your soldiers. Tell Pilate that Jesus' disciples came and stole the body while you were sleeping."

Longinus didn't respond but continued to stride as fast as he could toward Pilate's quarters.

"Wait," they implored. "At least share with Caiaphas what happened. *Then* make your report to Pilate. We'll vouch for you with Pilate. We're all in this together. You too. You pierced him. You were in charge on the hill."

The Centurion

While Longinus had little respect for the group, he did want to see Caiaphas's reaction, so he agreed to go with them and tell the high priest what happened.

When the group entered the court of Caiaphas, he was already there with a knot of others, who were waving their hands and describing the great light they had seen in the vicinity of the tombs. When Caiaphas saw Longinus, he hushed the rest of the people and said, "Centurion, you were there. Tell us, please, what happened."

"You know what happened," Longinus replied. "It happened just as he said it would. He came out of the tomb alive. The messenger of light from the sky called him the 'Son of God,' just as I did. That's what happened. Now, I will report to Pilate."

"No, wait—I must go with you," responded Caiaphas.

"Do as you will, but don't get in my way or delay me," Longinus said as his hand closed around the hilt of his sword. The message was clear.

Longinus strode through the door, the people around him scattering like pigeons on the pavement as he whisked briskly past them.

When Longinus got to Pilate's quarters, the whole place was buzzing with concern. The earthquake had terrified everyone. It was another omen.

The detachment from the tomb were already there, and Caiaphas and his entourage arrived shortly. Caiaphas's men busied themselves talking to the soldiers who'd been on the guard detail and giving them handfuls of silver coins as well as mouthfuls of words for Pilate.

Pilate motioned for Longinus to come into his private chambers. Caiaphas stepped forward to join the conversation, but Pilate cut him off with a wave of his hand. He said, "I didn't invite you. We'll talk after I have had a report from my centurion. Don't leave the tower. Stand right there."

Caiaphas did as he was ordered. He looked as white as Pilate's toga.

Pilate's eyes showed fear as they darted back and forth—as if he expected Jesus to walk in at any moment. He said, "Tell me, Longinus, what happened?"

Longinus told Pilate exactly what took place, and Pilate slumped down in his chair like a child being reprimanded by his father. All the color drained from his face, and he looked very much like a dead man, or one who would die soon.

"She was right," he muttered. "Claudia Procula was right. I should have listened to her. She said the gods had warned her, and she tried to warn me—"

"Sir," Longinus said, interrupting Pilate's trancelike state, "you promised me that I could leave with my wife when this detail was done. I ask your permission to do so."

"Yes, of course. Go. She'll be worried about you," Pilate answered vacantly.

"One more thing, sir," Longinus said. "The high priest and temple rulers have offered us money to say we were sleeping and that Jesus' disciples came and stole the body. I know the truth, and you know it too. Jesus came out of that tomb alive. No one stole his body."

"Yes, I know that," Pilate responded. "No harm will come to your soldiers. Let them have all the coins the priests can give them. Let them say what they will. We know the truth." Then he said, his voice trailing off, "Truth—what is truth?"

Longinus left the tower and rushed to Julius's home as fast as he could. Julia saw him coming and ran to meet him, tears streaming down her cheeks. "Oh, Longinus," she said, "I was so afraid for you. I saw the light, like a comet coming out of the sky, and it went to where you were. I was so afraid! What happened?"

Julius and Livia had dashed out to meet Longinus too. When they got into Julius's house and sat down, Longinus described in detail what happened. Julia, Livia, and Julius listened intently, nodding their acceptance of Longinus's story about what he had seen and heard. While they were awed, they seemed not to be surprised by what he told them. That puzzled him, and he asked them about it.

Julius cleared his throat and then spoke, "Longinus, the fact that Jesus is alive doesn't surprise us. He said that would happen, and we—all three of us—believed it would happen as he said it would. We spent all of last night studying the scrolls of the Hebrew prophets, and we believe that Jesus is who you said he is—the Son of God."

" 'We'?" questioned Longinus as he looked at Julia.

"Yes, me too," Julia said. "And there is more."

"More? What else?" Longinus asked in shock.

"You remember that before Gaius's accident he spent several weeks with us here in Jerusalem," Livia said.

"Yes, I remember, but—"

Livia held up her hand and then continued. "Gaius wanted to see Jerusalem, so we sent him out with Pulcher, who was also visiting us from Capernaum. Pulcher told Gaius about his being healed by Jesus, and Gaius insisted on meeting Jesus. So Pulcher took him to the home of one of Jesus' disciples. Gaius and Jesus talked about an hour or more. When Pulcher and he returned, Gaius asked us what we knew about Jesus, so we told him what we knew."

"I don't understand where this is going," said Longinus.

"Then listen, my love," soothed Julia.

Livia continued. "Gaius was a bright lad. He began to study the scrolls of the Hebrew prophets, and he compared what he read with what Jesus had told him. He found that the two harmonized perfectly. And—" Livia stopped, as she looked up at Longinus.

"And what?" asked Longinus.

"And Gaius announced to us that he believed Jesus to be the Messiah. Not only the Messiah of the Jews but of all people—Romans too."

Longinus was stunned.

Julia's soft voice broke the silence. "Jesus taught that those who believe in him will come back to life through the same power that raised him from the dead. Longinus, our son believed in Jesus as the Messiah. He believed, and the three of us believe too. We believe we will see Gaius again just as you saw Jesus come out of the grave—picked up from the ground by his Father."

Longinus knew how to fight a battle in hatred, but he didn't know how to fight this kind of battle. It was a battle waged in love and truth. Then he remembered Aquinas's words: *Follow your heart . . .*

After a moment to clear his thoughts, Longinus stood up, embraced Julia, and whispered, "I believe too. He is who I said he was—he is the Son of God. I believe too."

* * * * *

Julia and Longinus soon left for their home in Caesarea, where they would plan their long-awaited "new beginnings" trip. They had many things to discuss. This new part of their life together was like the military's wax-plated *tabula* when it had been exposed to the sun. It was a *tabula rasa*—a clean slate, ready for them to write their future. However, it wasn't the heat of the sun that made the difference, but the warmth of the Son.

A *tabula,* or writing tablet, consisted of two hollowed wooden frames filled with charcoal-darkened beeswax. A bronze stylus would be used to write in the wax. The writing was cleared for re-use by melting the wax with the heat of a flame or of the sun.

Questions for Thought and Discussion

When Pilate put Jesus on trial, he asked three penetrating and important questions. He asked Jesus, "Are you a king?" and "What is truth?" And then he asked the mob, "What shall I do with Jesus?"

These three questions, slightly revised, sum it all up. Everything—*everything,* including your inner peace and what will become of you in eternity—rests on how you answer these questions.

Is Jesus your King?

Is Jesus your truth?

What will *you* do with Jesus?

"Follow your heart . . ."